W9-AFL-036

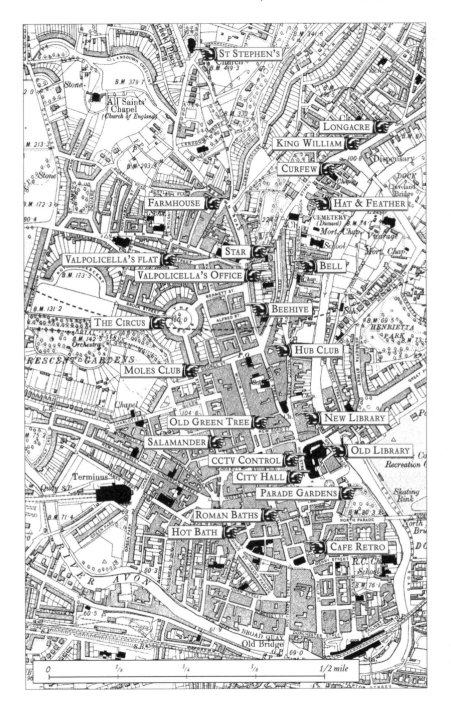

CATACOMBS OF TERROR!

CATACOMBS OF TERROR!

STANLEY DONWOOD

TYRUS
BOOKS

Copyright © 2015 by Stanley Donwood.
Originally published in the United Kingdom.
First U.S. printing, 2016, Tyrus Books.
All rights reserved.
This book, or parts thereof, may not be reproduced in any form without permission from the
publisher; exceptions are made for brief excerpts used in published reviews.

Published by
TYRUS BOOKS
an imprint of F+W Media, Inc.
10151 Carver Road, Suite 200
Blue Ash, OH 45242. U.S.A.
www.tyrusbooks.com

ISBN 10: 1-4405-9669-7
ISBN 13: 978-1-4405-9669-8
eISBN 10: 1-4405-9670-0
eISBN 13: 978-1-4405-9670-4

Printed in the United States of America.

10 9 8 7 6 5 4 3 2 1

Library of Congress Cataloging-in-Publication Data

Donwood, Stanley, author.
Catacombs of terror! / Stanley Donwood.
Blue Ash, OH: Tyrus Books, [2016]
LCCN 2016001979 (print) | LCCN 2016011432 (ebook) | ISBN 9781440596698 (hc) |
ISBN 1440596697 (hc) | ISBN 9781440596704 (ebook) | ISBN 1440596700 (ebook)
LCSH: Private investigators--Fiction. | Bath (England)--Fiction. | Detective and mystery fiction.
LCC PR6104.O59 C38 2016 (print) | LCC PR6104.O59 (ebook) | DDC 823/.92--dc23
LC record available at http://lccn.loc.gov/2016001979

Cover illustration and design by Chris Hopewell (Jacknife Design).
Author photo © Jake Green.

This book is available at quantity discounts for bulk purchases.
For information, please call 1-800-289-0963.

INTRODUCTION

The book you hold in your hands should not exist. By rights the manuscript should have taken flame and turned to ashes, high on Solsbury Hill in Somerset. It has a strange and convoluted history, which is only now, more than a decade after it was written, coming to light. If you are willing, I will take you back in time, to the early years of this century.

It was some time during the interminably hot summer of 2003 that I was approached by a publisher called Ambrose Blimfield, who had, he stated, a manuscript that I may be interested in acquiring. At the time I was the owner of an antiquarian bookshop in the city of Bath, and the manuscript, entitled *Catacombs of Terror!* was, Blimfield told me, set exclusively within and around that city. Rather excitedly, he insisted that the contents of the book would shake Bath to its core, forever demolishing the rather genteel fascination with the novels of Jane Austen then prevailing in the city—if only people could read it.

I was at a loose end, had no pressing engagements, and so I opened a bottle of Bordeaux and invited Blimfield to join me in a glass or two, and to tell me a little about this manuscript.

Catacombs had been written, he told me, as a result of a bet between Blimfield himself and an artist then living locally named Stanley Donwood, a bet laid on the night of the millennium. At the time Blimfield owned a publishing house called Hedonist Press, printing slender volumes of poetry and prose, although financial difficulties had driven him latterly to publish cheap pamphlets of erotica. Donwood had lately accrued some small degree of repute, creating record sleeves for pop groups, and had met Blimfield whilst carousing in one of Bath's seedier pubs, the Bell in Walcot Street.

Somehow a cider-fuelled bet had been laid between publisher and artist; and Ambrose Blimfield agreed to pay Donwood a handsome royalty if the latter could write a sixty-thousand-word detective novel in one month. The artist accepted, and amazingly, won the bet—*Catacombs of Terror!* was the result.

As Blimfield forcefully put it, the book was staggering. Set entirely locally, in and around the city of Bath, the novel was indeed a detective novel, a 'page-turner,' a 'blockbuster,' a 'gripping, unputdownable' thriller detailing the exploits of private eye Martin Valpolicella, as he battled through a single weekend of guns, drugs, and pigs. The book also drew heavily on some rather arcane research that Donwood had undertaken, research that hinted at a deeply unsavoury side to the city of Bath. Blimfield conceded that the book's style was somewhat slapdash, veering into cliché almost continually, sloppily written and falling far short of any conceivable literary merit.

On one hand the book marked a pinnacle of Blimfield's publishing career, and on the other it finished him off. He never published a book again, and retired bitter and cynical from the book publishing business.

His attempts to promote the book through bookshops, distribution channels, and direct to the public were plagued with disappointment, argument, legal disputes, and were ultimately doomed to almost complete failure.

In the meantime there were production issues with the book itself. The hemp paper that Blimfield insisted on for all his publications had been difficult to procure, and unreliable in use; the printing of *Catacombs* had been interrupted when the printers discovered sheets with holes in them. The replacement consignment was sound and the books finally printed, but this proved to be the last useable hemp paper ever dispatched from the mill. Its pioneering creator, John Hanson, mysteriously disappeared from his Dorset headquarters shortly afterwards, leaving no forwarding address. And none of the legendary 'tree-free' paper either. Blimfield's repeated attempts to trace him proved fruitless.

The Hedonist Press had lost its source of paper on which to print. While other publishers depended on authors, Blimfield's operation depended on hemp. He admitted to me that he didn't mind so much about the content of his books, it was what they were made of that counted. His publishing motto was *Hoc Excreta Bovis Possit, Mineme Non Aborious Factum Est* (sic), which supposedly translated as 'It may be bullshit but at least we didn't cut down any trees.' With no hemp, only woodpulp material remained, and Blimfield was stuck until someone was making hemp paper again. And this, in the early years of the twenty-first century, seemed extremely unlikely.

The stock of hemp paper that Blimfield possessed was enough to print a scant one thousand copies of *Catacombs*, provided that he set the type small and kept the margins narrow. The novel was eventually published in 2002, by which time Stanley Donwood had moved to London to pursue his artistic ambitions. While Internet sales of the books were steady, Blimfield remained disenchanted, occasionally muttering, "A book isn't a real book until it's in a bookshop," and insisting "Oxfam doesn't count." Eventually he took the entire remaining stock of the books to the neighbouring city of Bristol to try the retailing opportunities there—but promptly lost them somewhere in the city's Stokes Croft area.

It was time for Ambrose Blimfield to contact Stanley Donwood. There were no royalties to pay him—the book had actually lost Blimfield a considerable sum—but Blimfield was, by this time, part owner of a cider-apple orchard and decided to pay Donwood in cider. The pair agreed to meet on the top of Solsbury Hill on the outskirts of Bath.

It was at this point in his account that Blimfield began avoiding my eye. His enthusiasm for his tale seemed to wane. But I refilled his glass and gestured for him to continue.

Solsbury Hill rises more than six hundred feet above sea level, and lies to the east of Bath. For Blimfield it was a weary climb on a hot afternoon, carrying a great deal of cider. When he arrived at last at the summit, he saw that Stanley Donwood was already there, leaning against a concrete triangulation point, looking down over the city.

Donwood, it appeared, had not forgotten about *Catacombs*—far from it. During his sojourn in London he had returned repeatedly to the manuscript, which he now presented once more to Blimfield. He had corrected it, he had edited it, he had made it better. Blimfield told me that he was once again presented with the manuscript of *Catacombs of Terror!*—a dog-eared ream of A4 pages, stained with coffee, wine, and grime, heavily annotated, with paragraphs crossed out, scrawled handwriting crowding the margins—and yes, from a perfunctory reading of the initial pages, it did indeed seem to be a superior job to the original. The two of them spent several hours drinking cider and smoking marijuana as the sun set over the city of Bath below them, their conversation sometimes turning to the fortune they would make with this rewritten masterpiece, sometimes to the futility of writing, of publishing, of life itself.

They lit a small fire as twilight enveloped the hill. By now they were both quite drunk. Blimfield says that Donwood had fallen silent, merely nodding as the publisher expostulated upon the iniquities of vested interests in the print trade, on the emergence of Amazon, and on the insurmountable difficulties facing those in the book trade. Apparently at some later stage, after stumbling to his feet, Donwood uttered a terrible shriek and threw his precious manuscript into the fire, before collapsing to the ground, insensible.

Blimfield made some attempts to rouse the artist, but received only abuse for his efforts. It was then that his gaze turned to the manuscript smouldering on the fire, flames licking at the dog-eared pages. He made a decision at that moment. With a glance at the snoring Donwood, he seized the burning bundle of papers and pulled it from the fire, patting out the creeping combustion with his bare hands, smacking the manuscript on the grass.

Blimfield told me that he didn't really know what he was doing, that he couldn't be held fully responsible for his actions due to the amount of cider they had drunk—but he made the decision that the manuscript could not be lost.

He draped his jacket over the slumbering Donwood, left the remains of the cider next to him, and 'practically fell' down the steep side of Solsbury Hill. He claimed to remember nothing of the rest of the night, and was awoken, still clutching the sooty manuscript, the next morning by the cleaner of the Bell in Walcot Street, who asked him what he was doing sleeping in the toilet cubicle.

I asked Blimfield if he had seen Donwood since that night on Solsbury Hill, and he shook his head. The two had exchanged letters, postcards, and the occasional e-mail, but Donwood, having returned to London, had remained under the impression that he had destroyed the only copy of the manuscript of *Catacombs of Terror!*, that he had thrown it, drunkenly, into a fire. According to Blimfield he had said that it was 'probably for the best.' Apparently Donwood had 'form' in this sort of behaviour, having destroyed a novel entitled *Yobs* that he had written on the grounds that it was 'too violent.'

The manuscript that Blimfield was offering me did fit with the description given. It was of about four hundred sheets of A4, bundled with elastic bands, scorched at the edges, stained, enthusiastically annotated, and entitled *Catacombs of Terror!* The exclamation mark, said Blimfield, was very important. Blimfield himself had indeed forsaken the world of book publishing, and was now in the newspaper business, and proposed to purchase a decommissioned milk float, in order to travel the country publishing local newspapers, written by an 'acquaintance' of his. It was to raise funds for this venture that he wished to sell me the manuscript.

By now our bottle of wine was empty, but Blimfield's story had intrigued me. I opened another bottle and we began to discuss a price. To be fair, I had no real reason to buy the manuscript, but now I felt that I simply had to read it, and at the time—oh, those balmy days at the start of the century—I was comparatively well off. Of which more shortly. As far as I understood the story, there had been a thousand copies of the first draft of *Catacombs* published, some of which had been sold, some of which had been lost. There was no electronic copy of the text, the computers belonging to Hedonist Press having long been consigned to landfill. The only extant copy of the manuscript—an edited, corrected version—lay on the desk between us.

That hot afternoon drew on, and Blimfield enthused about his milk float and about the dire need, as he saw it, for genuinely local daily newspapers, and about the ability of his business partner to write these newspapers with very little knowledge of local matters. This new acquaintance, it appeared, was also willing to be paid in cider. I kept my considerable reservations about all of this to myself, and, as the second bottle was finished, we agreed on a price; I paid Blimfield, and, as it happened, that was the last I saw of him. I wished him well with his milk float, his nascent newspaper empire, and thought little of the matter for the next decade. The manuscript, all but forgotten, languished in my desk drawer—until 2014.

The foregoing is by way of a preamble, some background to explain how you, the reader, happens to be reading *Catacombs of Terror!* As I say, in 2003 I was the proprietor of a small antiquarian bookshop in Bath—and that was the trade I plied for some years after. I put the manuscript away for safe-keeping, and concentrated on my shop, on buying and selling, on book fairs, rumours of rare first editions, on calfskin bindings, disputed titles verso, on 'slight foxing' and 'signs of wear.' But to my dismay, the real world, as it likes to be known, came knocking. Publishing houses such as Wordsworth began to print cheap editions of the classics—and thus I lost the casual trade of the students looking for serviceable copies of Shakespeare, Dickens, Thackeray, and the like. Then the Internet began to take chunks from my market—who would browse my dusty shop when they could type in a title on their personal computer and buy the edition they chose from a host of sellers worldwide at the click of a mouse?

The shops that neighboured mine closed one by one, replaced by estate agents and outlets offering overpriced coffee, with 'boutique pop-ups' which appeared to sell nothing very much at all. It was a slow process, almost imperceptible, but my shop became untenable. My lifestyle—late rising, a glass of wine or two at lunch, amiable conversations with fellow bibliophiles—became untenable. With great regret, I closed my shop, and announced to my landlord that I would not be renewing my lease.

Whilst engaged in the desultory process of clearing out my shop I came across the—almost forgotten—manuscript that I had bought from the publisher Ambrose Blimfield a full decade previously. The whole tale came, unbidden, back to me. And I thought to myself—perhaps now is the time to 'cash in' on my investment?

One does not run an antiquarian bookshop for twenty-five years or more without making friends, and recently I had been spending some time with a very good friend who shared much of my dismay at the way that things had changed, the way things were not as they used to be, particularly in the world of books.

The publishing house of Scratter & Pomace was founded in 1888 by Alfred Scratter and Juan Pomace, and for many years was highly regarded in the book trade. Notably, the now classic *A Pedlar's Tale* by Devlin Crease was published by that house to great acclaim at the turn of the century, and their deftly chosen list was envied by many. During the second half of the twentieth century they fought hard to avoid being subsumed into the great conglomerates, jackals such as HarperCollins, Penguin Random House, and the like.

In hindsight this may have been something of a tactical error, as it turned out that the very same economic forces that brought low my own little shop had also unhorsed the venerable firm of Scratter & Pomace—cheap reprints of out-of-copyright classics, Amazon's dominance of the market, and so on.

Richard Scratter, the great-grandson of Alfred, was my very good friend. And it was to him that I turned. The glory days of deluxe hardback editions, it was apparent, were in the past. S&P had fallen sufficiently low for them to be competing with the likes of Wordsworth on cheap reprints of *Treasure Island, Tess of the*

D'Urbervilles, and suchlike. Richard was contemplating the fate of other publishers he knew who had been reduced to printing anthologies of what is apparently termed 'bottle-creep'—amateur erotica reprinted from Internet sources, where like-minded perverts would share and mutually appreciate appallingly written screeds of sexual fantasies.

Scratter and I discussed the possibility of publishing *Catacombs of Terror!* as a mass-market paperback, and over lunch in a delightful restaurant we made an agreement. He would engage a professional to retype the manuscript, and a highly proficient illustrator to produce cover art, and *Catacombs* would live again.

I thought again of the tale that Ambrose Blimfield had told me—that story of a bet, of a book, of publishing books on hemp paper, of fire, of drunkenness, and I thought—this book *should* live again.

Once Carol, our typist, had transcribed the damaged manuscript, Scratter and myself read it through—and we were fascinated. Somehow the writer had recast the city of Bath—'a genteel tourist trap,' as it's described in the book—as the setting for an infernal drama played out in the sombre, rain-soaked tones of a horror story. The text is littered with swear words, there is frequent reference to illegal drugs, several lines appear to be lifted verbatim from more famous detective novels, names are stolen from other books, and, notably, from a little-known document called the *Neoist Manifestos*, and a sort of cod-Esperanto is employed as an archaic language, but remarkably, none of this seems to matter.

I looked up Stanley Donwood on the Internet and sent a letter to his agent. Soon enough, a reply arrived stating that Donwood had very little recollection of the book and even less desire to have anything to do with it—in fact, he apparently disowned it, much as he had disowned *Yobs*—and he wished us 'the best of luck with that cheap trash.'

However, as you will discover in the following pages, *Catacombs of Terror!* is anything but cheap trash. Is it trashy? Well, perhaps. Is it a 'page-turner'? Undoubtedly. And thrilling? Undeniably. And even if it captures a time now passed—a world of slow modems, of smoking in pubs and cafés, of dictaphones and tape recorders, a world when surveillance was new enough to be remarked upon—the book resonates. The plucky individual, flawed, but still, at root, deeply moral, fighting against a world that shows no mercy, that confounds him at every turn, fighting against the inevitability of defeat, buoyed by the merest hint of love . . . this dark account of a terrible weekend in the beautiful city of Bath compels us to look beyond the facade. It takes us to the underground, behind the curtain, beneath the polite, respectable veil that society would draw across the horrors that lie beneath. It takes us down . . . down to the Catacombs of Terror!

—Sterling Bland, Bath, 2015

CHAPTER 1

DEATH THREATS

Let's see. Friday 10th July, 11:30 A.M. Not a good time for me, and not a good day either, so far. Not if you were me. The best thing about my situation was that I'd escaped the wind. And the rain. The cold was still with me, but I was forgetting it fast. I'd delegated. A third coffee was dealing with it. The worst thing about my situation you don't want to know. Yeah, well. I didn't know the worst thing about my situation either. Not yet, anyway.

July. The coldest and wettest ever, I thought. Okay. But I thought that every year. Maybe it was getting worse, every year. The sky squatted above the city, snagging on the chimneys and aerials, sagging into the streets like a wet military blanket. I lit my fourth cigarette since escaping the downpour and tried to focus on the newspaper I had propped in front of me. The usual. Imminent terrors, tawdry killings, economic gloom. I wasn't feeling too good.

I put my coffee cup down and stared out at the rain. I had enough available overdraft to pay this month's rent, but apart from that I was looking at a series of humiliating, embarrassing, and finally futile phone calls to my bank manager. Brown envelopes through the door en route to the wastepaper basket. Reminders, ditto. Final demands. Bailiffs. Then what?

I still hadn't been paid for my last job. Or the one before that. My first couple of years as a private investigator had gone okay. Dull, but okay. But this year had been dead. Three cases, all of them very boring. Identify, tail, photograph, deliver prints. And my last two clients had defaulted. Hadn't returned my increasingly frequent phone calls. I'd started considering employing a debt collector. Not my favourite kind of people, having been on the receiving end of their kind more than once. It wasn't a global crisis, I thought, looking briefly at the headlines. But it wasn't any kind of fun. It was enough. And Barry Eliot? He was more than enough. The guy was not necessary.

Well, okay. Maybe the Barry Eliot problem was my fault. Partly my fault. About one third my fault, I reckoned. Half my fault would be pushing it . . . maybe. All right. I'd met Karen Eliot the night before. Again. I had been on my way home after a busy day watching the telephone, fiddling with paper clips, reading a magazine. A quick drink? Sure, why not. A bite to eat? Well, I had nothing much to look forward to in my fridge back at the flat, so, hey, why not. Well, okay. Barry's away. You're lonely. Sure. And then I'd woken up in the morning, Friday 10th July, in her bed. Groggy, hung over, and with the horribly dawning realisation that I'd done it again. I'd spent the night with Karen. Again.

It had been only two weeks since Barry had caught us in bed, one stupid afternoon when he was supposed to be playing golf with some of those high fliers he likes so much. He'd probably suspected something was going on. Karen and me—we really got on well. And I mean it. She hated Barry. She liked me. And maybe more than liked. I felt—well, I felt that we could have had some kind of life together. In another world. Another life. Some other dimension. Anyway. Barry had walked in. It wasn't a good moment, not compared with the moment just before.

He threatened to kill me—yawn—and then threatened to have my licence revoked. Okay. Death threats from Barry, with his squeaking voice and appalling taste in golfing slacks I could handle, but losing my licence . . . .

The trouble was that Barry was extremely well connected. I didn't know why, but he was. He knew people in the Council. He knew people in the police force. I mean, the guy played *golf*. He put on those revolting slacks, those sickening pullovers, those laughable shoes—and schmoozed in the nineteenth hole with magistrates, judges, superintendents, and commissioners. He had his gig sewn up. If Barry wanted, Barry usually got. He was, you could be forgiven for thinking, not a guy to cross. And I was screwing his wife. Maybe I was in love with her. I didn't know. I couldn't tell.

You see? That was the worst thing about my situation. As I thought then, as I shouldered my way out of the café and into the weather. Yeah. As I thought then.

CHAPTER 2

OH FUCK YOU

It was nearly midday, and if I didn't at least sit behind my desk for a few minutes I couldn't justify lunch. I decided to look up debt collection services in the Yellow Pages. Time to hit the office. Ha. Won't you step through to my office? Step along the alleyway past the dog shit, the puke slicks, the garbage, the never-picked-up bin liners, their contents spewed along the concrete. Come through the peeling, flaking door along the corridor that always, inexplicably, smells of human piss. I'll just unlock the door. Notice the brass plaque on your way in? Not as shiny as maybe it could have been, but still. *VALPOLICELLA INVESTIGATIONS*. Yep, that's me. The boss. Martin Valpolicella. Got a problem? Missing husband? Missing wife? Missing cat? You've come to the right place. Oh, for sure.

I let myself into the office and clicked the light on and picked a piece of paper off the mat. A note, written in block biro letters on good-quality paper. Before I read it, I dropped the note on my desk. I walked over to the cupboard, opened it, grabbed a bottle, and poured myself two fingers of whiskey. I sat down behind my desk and fumbled in my pocket for my cigarettes.

So, it's either good news—like a job, for example. Any other kind of good news was pretty much inconceivable. A job. That would be very good. I needed a job badly, it was true. Or else it's bad news. Which I felt was definitely more likely. Bad news could come in a number of ways, but it was pretty unlikely that really, seriously bad news could come in the form of a note. A note, at least, delayed the worst of the news. I was glad that I'd thought that through. The note was going to be okay. I reached across and picked it up.

CITY BATHS
13 JULY AM

Not bad. Incomprehensible, but not dangerous. It wasn't bad news. Not yet. I turned the paper over.

YOU'RE BEING SET UP
valpolicellaneedtoknowthis@yahoo.com

Still not bad news, strictly speaking. Unsettling, yes. Unwelcome? Check. The kind of communication that made me wish I'd skipped the office and gone straight into lunch? Yeah, well. Maybe lunch didn't look so good anymore. My headache was coming back. Wearily I stooped down and plugged in the power cable for the computer, swapped phone jacks, and started up. Again, I decided to get a faster modem. What would you have done if you had the misfortune to be me? You would have ignored it. That would have been your response, right? You're lucky. You're not me.

I hit 'compose' and typed *oh fuck you*. Kicked over a chair. Shrugged. Took a couple of Rennies and went to lunch anyway.

CHAPTER 3

MY STUPID JOB

It must have been the wine, but when I got back, despite my saner instincts I went through the over-familiar Internet connection rigmarole and guess what? I had mail. A reply, no less. Of course. Lunch, however long you spend on it, however much it costs, doesn't stop anything from happening.

> Oh yeah? Valpolicella you need to know this
> You are being set up
> You are the fall guy for 13 July by fate ordained
> I don't like you but if you're scared enough you might be able to stop it
> Valpolicella go to the star at 7 pm talk to jeans with a hole at each knee

Okay. It was only three. I had time to think. *Set up? Fall guy?* This whole thing stunk of Barry. Some sort of stupid golfer's bullshit with the aim of giving me the runaround and probably a good kicking as a finale. The 13th July? Couple of days' time. The date was probably a red herring, a little bit of bait to make this sound slightly more interesting than it actually was.

If it *was* Barry, he obviously wanted to see me sweat for a while. He had the time and the twisted sort of energy to do something like this. Okay. He had reason to dislike me, and he knew where I plied my trade. My name was on the plaque. I mentioned that before. But it was the *I don't like you* that intrigued me. Would Barry need to actually state that he didn't like me? I knew all too well that the fucker didn't like me. *I don't like you but if you're scared enough you might be able to stop it.* Stop what, for fuck's sake? Stop smoking? Stop myself from throwing the computer out the window?

I made myself an instant coffee and leaned back, gazing at the sagging cobwebs of dust that hung from the picture rail. The coffee was horrible, as usual. I tried to think. I might have been mistaken, but it seemed to me that I knew nothing at all about any of this apart from two things. First, I was apparently being set up to take the rap for something—something unspecified— that was apparently due to happen in, what, three days' time. Second, if I went and talked to a guy with holes in his trousers, things might turn out fine. It might be a setup. Yeah, well. Some kind of hilarious joke from a golfer who'd had his ego deflated. Or it might actually turn out to be a job. It might even be a paid job. The idea kind of interested me. Anyway. The only star I knew was the Star, a pub not too far from my office.

I watched the phone for a while, then I played about with the stapler. The afternoon began to pall, so I decided to get to the Star early. Heavy traffic was heading east and the rain had decided to stick around, make itself at home, get comfortable. I climbed up some steps from the street where my office was and turned towards the Star, pulling up my collar, huddling my shoulders against the wind. I couldn't help thinking about my life. My stupid job. My finances. This fucking city.

I had a couple of drinks at the bar and, frankly, I was becoming ever so slightly bored by the time a woman came in, jeans, hole at each knee. Somehow I hadn't been expecting a woman. That surprised me, and I don't surprise that easily, as a rule. She was small, brown hair, denim jacket. About twenty-five. I wouldn't have noticed her in a crowd. She seemed to notice me, though. She walked up to me.

"Hi. Are you Mister Valpolicella?" She had quite a refined voice. Home counties.

"Mmhmm," I said quietly. "I'm Valpolicella. Who are you?"

She looked at me just long enough to register disdain, then nodded towards the bar.

"Red wine. Best they've got. Large glass. See you over there." The girl gestured to a corner table and headed towards it. I got the drinks and walked over to the table with a glass of house red for her and a pint of lager for me. I looked at her. I have different ways of looking at people for different situations. This situation called for my 'do not dare to waste my time' look. It's partly glare, partly stare, mostly bored, without a hint of smile. It's usually best to follow this look with a disguised insult.

"So, what's a nice girl like you doing in a place like this?"

"You do know that I'm just here to relay a message? That I have no interest in you, or your life, whatsoever?" she said. I sat down at the table and leant forward.

"Uh huh. Now we've got the pleasantries over with, let's suppose we can get down to business. You tell me what you're here to tell me, and I'll think about it. I'm not remotely happy about any of this. Is this a job? Or a magical mystery tour? And, most importantly, do I get paid?"

She looked down at her shoes and then up at me, slowly. I stared at her. I was perplexed. More than perplexed, I was annoyed. A note? An e-mail? An unknown woman in a city pub? This was adding up towards a total I couldn't imagine. And somewhere inside it was a time limit. Three days. No, pretty much only two days. I thought of walking away. Just getting up, walking away. Maybe that's what you would have done. I should have done it, too. I really should. But I didn't. Yeah, well.

"So?"

She looked up at the ceiling. The Star is an old-fashioned kind of place. No jukebox, no games machines. Lots of dark wood and lots of little rooms. It was the kind of place that, if it was early in the evening, you could be alone. Which is what we were, as far as I could tell. She looked up at the nicotine-stained ceiling for a slow minute before she spoke.

"Are you recording this?" she asked, eyes narrow.

It was my turn to inspect the ceiling, although I took a lot less time than her.

"No, I'm not recording this. I'm here because something about this business interested me. If it stops interesting me, I'm gone. Bye-bye Valpolicella. What in hell would I be recording? And why?" I took a pull on my pint.

"I'm just talking. Talking to a detective. Isn't that what you're supposed to be, Mister Valpolicella? I wouldn't like what I'm going to say to find its way into the wrong ears. Careless talk . . . can cost lives, Mister Valpolicella."

"Yeah." I was getting exasperated. "You going to talk or are we going to sit here breaking ice?"

"I'm going to talk, Mister Valpolicella, and I think you should listen. You might think you know this city, but you don't. It doesn't seem like the kind of city where much goes on. A genteel tourist trap. I wonder how you stay in business. Grimly, and rather desperately, I would imagine. Divorce cases. Domestic spying. Rather insalubrious. You live in this city, but you don't really know what's happening beneath the surface. I'm not surprised. Hardly anybody knows what's going on here. I know. I know that you're going to be arrested on the afternoon of Monday 13th July. For murder."

I was suddenly listening. I was suddenly listening hard.

"And I assume that you would rather that didn't happen. That you would rather carry on with your life, your busy life, in your usual way. No clients. Terrible address. Worse reputation. Ignorant. But free. So I have some information for you that might—just might—enable you to stay here, among the innocent, the ignorant, and the free. Now, on the morning of the 13th July, before the tourists arrive, something—someone—will be found in the city Baths. The Baths will have to be closed. The police will be called. The city's biggest tourist attraction is the Baths. The reason why this city is here, some would say. What the city does not want to find in the Baths is a dismembered corpse, Mister Valpolicella. The legs will be found on the west pediment. The arms on the north and south. The torso will be weighted and sunk to the bottom of the water itself. It might take a while for it to be found, but its location could, presumably, be deduced from the fact that the head will be found on the east pediment. Staring up at the sky." She paused, took a sip from her glass, and looked directly at me. "This city, this city that you live and work in but know so little about, will not shrug its shoulders. This city will demand a culprit. And you, Mister Valpolicella, will be that culprit. The villain of the piece."

I was feeling just a little unsettled, but I wasn't about to let this girl know that.

"Pretty speech. You still haven't told me who you are. And this isn't the first time I've had someone bullshit me in a pub." I lit a cigarette. Slowly. "Give me one reason why I should take this at all seriously."

"Because it's true."

"It doesn't sound true."

"I'm trying to help you, Mister Valpolicella."

The *Mister* was beginning to grate. Her voice was beginning to grate. I began thinking about leaving, or at least getting another pint. Okay. I shot her a glance and stood up.

"You're trying to help me," I said, exhaling. "You're trying to help me, and that's very nice. You know what? My bank manager says he's trying to help me as well, but I'm not about to take him entirely seriously. Do me a favour. Look at this from my angle. I get a note, anonymously. I get an e-mail, also anonymously, telling me to come here. Meet you. Well, that's great. It's been real. A diverting evening."

"Do you want another drink, Mister Valpolicella?"

"If you drop the *Mister*."

She went over to the bar. I sat down and ground out my cigarette in the ashtray. I lit another and stared into space. The wood-panelled walls of the Star seemed to be closing in on me. I felt pinpricks of anxiety beginning to cluster round the back of my neck. I had the feeling that whatever this was leading up to was going to be unpleasant. I had a little time to think about different types of unpleasantness, but I tried not to get too involved. Then she came back over. She didn't have a drink for herself.

"Valpolicella, I'm not going to take up much more of your obviously valuable time."

I let that one go. She carried on.

"There's no point in trying to persuade you that I'm not lying to you. So there's just this. There's a lot at stake; not just your liberty." I had to stop her this time. I'd just remembered something that I should ask her about.

"How's Barry?" I interrupted.

"*Barry?*" she said, questioningly. I was perplexed. There were only two ways of hearing her say his name. One was hearing a very good actor pretending she'd never heard of any Barry. The other was hearing somebody who genuinely had no idea what I was talking about. She didn't know a Barry. The second way bothered me way more than the first.

"Barry Eliot. Hotshot. Entrepreneur. All-round influential guy. Plays golf. Probably doesn't like me too well." I said it wearily, which wasn't something I had any choice about. I was suddenly very tired.

"What the hell are you talking about, Valpolicella? Now, listen. There are some things you need to do as soon as possible. There's an archaeological dig up at a place called Charlcombe. It's in a rural valley, northeast of the city. Go there. Find out who's running it, find out what they're looking for. And you need to find out what they discovered when the same crew did a dig in the Circus. 1993. You know where the Circus is, I imagine?"

I nodded tersely. The Circus is a city tourist feature. A kind of primitive roundabout surrounded by big houses. Very popular with the snapshot and video camera nuts from all over.

"You could find out who's got the contract to run the city's CCTV network. And maybe you could go to a pub called the Old Green Tree at seven o'clock tomorrow evening. Meet someone in a Stonehenge T-shirt." She paused. Cleared her throat. "Or perhaps you'd like to ignore me. Do nothing. Wait for the police to arrive. And arrest you for murder. At about one P.M. on Monday, the 13th of July. Perhaps *that's* what you'd like to do."

She was staring at me, willing me to understand, to remember, to act. I looked straight back, into her eyes. They were brown. I hadn't noticed before.

"Okay. Bye, Mister Valpolicella," she said. She turned.

"Hey! What's your name?" I said.

She was gone.

"Didn't get a name. Should always get a name," I said quietly to my drink. My drink didn't reply. So I drank it. Then I groaned. I sank my face into my hands. Nowhere had there been any mention of money.

CHAPTER 4

RATHER YOU THAN ME

Back at the office I broke some furniture. I put my foot through my coffee table, which was a mistake. It was worth money. I could have sold it, at least in theory. This realisation annoyed me, so I broke a chair. That was a mistake, too. I had only two chairs, which at least nominally provided seating for me plus a client. Now I had one chair. At least I still had a couch. I sat down on it heavily.

Where had this started? My brains needed racking, but I couldn't be bothered. I poured a whiskey and lit a cigarette. I grabbed a map from the shelf and looked up Charlcombe. Yep, northeast of the city. A lane looped around the valley. There were a few houses, a church. The easiest way to get there was to go up through the eastern suburbs. Archaeological digs? Give me strength. What had I done to deserve this? Okay. I was *Mister* Valpolicella. I was a professional. A private investigator. I had a licence. Well, for the time being anyway. No way was I going to be jerked around. Not without my consent. If there were strings to pull I was going to find them. And I was going to pull them.

It was after 10 p.m., and the rain still fell. It had been raining for my whole life. I walked along the street towards the Old Green Tree. Research. If I was going to meet some clown in a

Stonehenge T-shirt in there tomorrow night I wanted to find out if he was a regular. If anyone knew anything about him. The Old Green Tree was another old-fashioned wood-panelled place, but about a quarter the size of the Star. It was busy in there, but not so busy that a guy couldn't get a drink. So that's what I did.

"You work in here most nights?" I asked the barman. He was a tall guy. Didn't shave too carefully. Pierced left eyebrow.

He made a sound that could have been affirmative, could've been negative. He didn't look at me. He was busy, too, I guess. He had some glasses to wash. Beer mats to straighten. A very busy barman. But not so busy he couldn't answer a few polite questions.

"I'm supposed to be meeting someone in here," I pressed on. "Maybe you know—them?" It occurred to me that the girl who hadn't told me her name had also not told me whether I was supposed to meet a man or a woman. I decided to take another gamble. "Always wears this stupid T-shirt from Stonehenge. Ring any bells?"

The barman glanced up at me. He straightened a beer towel on the counter. Shook his head. Served someone else. Okay. I looked for somewhere to sit down. No dice. I drank my drink and pushed my way back to the bar.

"See you," I said cheerily to the barman as I put my empty glass down. Yeah, well. I'm a civilised guy.

"Thanks. Hey, wait a sec. Did you meet your friend? I think I know who you mean." I was taken by surprise. I was beginning to get used to the sensation.

"A no-show," I answered. "I think I might have got the wrong night." I knew damn well I had the wrong night. I was twenty-four hours early. "Why? Did you see, er, him?"

"Not tonight. He was in last night though. Maybe you did get the wrong night. Friend of yours, is he?" His question was asked with a hint of distaste. An undertone of disgust.

"Not strictly. A business acquaintance, perhaps."

"Rather you than me. Bye." He moved through to the other bar where a small pack of off-duty rugby players were getting restive. I took a look at my watch. I left. It wasn't warm outside, and it wasn't dry.

CHAPTER 5

LOW-RENT PHILIP MARLOWE

I needed to think. I walked the wet streets. And I realised that Friday night at closing time was not the kind of time to walk streets and think. The usual howling gangs of drunks weaved around, screaming like badly dressed baboons. I guess they were maybe on their way to refresh the puke slicks in the alleyway outside my office. Yeah, well. Someone had to do it, and I'd rather it didn't have to be me.

I pulled out my mobile and dialled a number. Colin Kafka was someone I knew from way back. We'd both become involved in some stuff, some stuff that wasn't strictly legit . . . fuck, it was out-and-out criminal. Kafka got unlucky. He was looking at spending the rest of his life staring at the sky through small windows with bars on them, watching his back, and waiting for appeals that would never have come. But I'd managed to get him—and myself—off the hook. Connections. That was when I still had them. In the past. In the old days. I could say the good old days, but I'd be lying. I hadn't seen or heard from Kafka for ten or fifteen years. Until recently.

He'd called me—out of the blue—and suggested that we meet up. Things had certainly changed, all right. I was an investigator and he was now a reporter on the local paper, both in the same city. Interesting coincidence, I'd thought. And Colin Kafka, of all people. A reporter now. A journalist. Anyway. We'd exchanged greetings. What a coincidence, small world—you know the kind of thing. I'd reluctantly taken his mobile number. Maybe we could meet up, go for a beer, act like regular old pals, pretend the past had never happened. Yeah, well. I made my excuses, said I was pretty busy. Tell the truth, I hadn't had much interest in seeing him. Or so I had thought. Now I thought differently.

"Colin? Colin Kafka? It's Martin Valpolicella. How about that drink?"

Kafka was out already, spending his salary at one of the all-night places on the east side of town. Okay. I was pretty much wet through, but the rain wasn't in any hurry to leave, so I hiked it back out of the city centre. My office was on the way, so I dropped by for something to warm me up. I flicked on the light, poured myself a whiskey, and sat behind my desk. I put my feet up. And I wondered, again, what the hell was going on. It seemed that someone—or some people—unknown wanted me to do a little dirt-digging for them. And for myself. I wondered why that woman had given me this ragbag of clues. They seemed like questions she already had the answers to. And if that was the case, why did I have to answer them all over again? Who was she? Had she sent the note and the e-mail? Or someone else? And what was the deal with the guy with the Stonehenge T-shirt? But the one thing that really bugged me was my fee. Or rather, the lack of it.

Rather you than me, the barman in the Old Green Tree had said. With that I agreed. Yeah, well. Wouldn't you? If you were me? Questions whirled around my head like angry wasps. I drank my whiskey. And had another.

I found Kafka in a late night joint off the London Road. It was about 1:30 A.M. by the time I got there. The place had a sign outside: *The Lud Club. Members only.* I mentioned Colin's name and I was in. Open sesame. He was obviously a regular. I walked over to the bar and ordered whiskey. While the barman was pouring, I took in the scene. Dingy, smoky, filled with huddled figures around tables. Talking deals, plans, violence to be meted out. What was it the girl in the Star had said about my job? Insalubrious. I'm good with words. A quick learner. This place was insalubrious. For sure. I had trouble spotting Colin. It was over a decade since I'd seen him last. The Kafka I knew, ten years ago, was a skinhead with his head in a book when it wasn't butting a cop. I scoped the joint and caught nothing answering that description. But then I saw him. Haircut that looked like it cost money. Clothes, ditto. Well, ten years. Everything is subject to change. He was nothing like the Kafka I remembered. He was practically unrecognisable. But I recognised him. Yeah, well. I've got a memory for a face, at least. If nothing else. If nothing else at all.

"Colin," I said, sitting down next to him. The guys he was with looked at him, asking questions with their eyes.

"Martin's an old friend," he said, perhaps a little too quickly. A little too nervously. "Haven't seen him for years."

The guys got up.

"Well, have . . . fun," one of them said, "reminiscing. Or whatever." They went across the room, giving me a backward glance wrapped round a sneer.

"Nice folks," I said to Kafka. "Friends?"

"Acquaintances. I'm doing a story on—well, unsavoury local characters. Vice stuff, petty crime, protection . . . . They're keen not to be associated with that kind of thing, but they'd like a certain other individual to feature highly in my exposé. So, um, we're working out a . . . deal." Colin looked flustered. I looked faintly disgusted, and let him register my expression.

"Nice. Very nice. I've always been a fan of the free press. Unbiased. Reliable. That sort of thing. But I'm not judgemental about people. I mean, I like criminals. They keep me in business. Well, anyway. You can get back to that sometime soon. I won't detain you unnecessarily. How are you? Long time now. A very long time."

"It's . . . good to see you, Martin. You look, well, you look bad. You look . . . like shit. I suppose you want something?" His fluster was turning to anger.

"Be nice, Colin. This hostile attitude is very last week, and I think we should be friends. It's true I want something. I've been told that I may be arrested after the weekend, and I'm sure you remember how I helped that from happening to you once upon a time."

I was sweetness itself. I was calm, cool, and collected.

"Martin. Okay. What do you want? How on earth can I stop you from getting arrested? I mean, what have you done?"

"I've done nothing. Well, nothing bad. Not recently. Nothing like murder. And that's what I'm apparently going to get fingered for. It's some kind of setup. I have a vague idea who may be behind it, but I think that I'm maybe wrong. Something is going on. Something very ugly. For some reason I'm involved. And I need to know what that something is and why I'm being picked to play patsy. Am I wrong to want to find these things out? Or am I right?"

Kafka looked at me carefully. His eyes glittered behind his glasses. Perhaps he was sensing a story. He was a hack now, after all. "Okay, Martin. Okay so far. It's true I owe you a favour. How would you like me to help you?"

"I want you to get me some information. It's simple. Do you have a pen? A notebook? A memory?"

Kafka gave me a glare that was now only five percent anger. I'd say it was eighty-five percent annoyance. The rest was boredom, or one of boredom's close relations. A mention of murder doesn't have much impact these days. Yeah, well.

"I have those, Martin. Particularly the last. What information do you want?"

"Well, there's an archaeological dig at Charlcombe, which is a country valley north of here. About a mile or two. If you could get me some details on that, I'd be happier than I am right now. I'm interested in that dig, for some reason. I'd like to know who's running it, and I'd like to find out what it is that they're looking for. For some reason. I'd like to know what they were looking for in the Circus in 1993. You know the Circus? It was the same group doing the dig there, as far as I know."

Kafka was writing in his notebook. This was probably the most encouraging thing that had happened to me all day. I looked at my watch. 2 A.M. Okay. I thought briefly about the wrap of coke back at the office. Yeah. I was going to be okay. No way was I getting arrested for a ritual murder in a premier tourist attraction. It would be problematic, to say the least. If it wasn't a crock of shit. And that was something that was still out with the jury. Kafka's next statement reminded me how far out the jury was.

"You come in here, in this club, acting like some extremely low-rent Philip Marlowe, and you want me to find out about archaeologists? Archaeologists. Why don't you just phone them? Shit, Valpolicella, how badly have you lost it?"

"I don't know. Possibly very badly. Possibly. But listen. I've been given a lot of questions and I'm suspicious of all of them.

What I want now is a lot of answers that I can be suspicious of. Make sense?"

"Mmm, I suppose. In a very strange way. Anything else, while I can still be bothered to write it down?"

I stared at him, for a moment doubting myself. I tried to remember everything that the woman in the Star had said.

"Yeah, well. There's one other thing. If it isn't too much . . . trouble. Could you find out who's got the contract to run the city's CCTV network?"

Kafka threw his gaze from his notebook to me. "I just might. How urgent is this?"

"Like I said, it seems I'm due to be arrested on Monday. For murder. Apparently. But, you know, it happens that I don't want to take any unnecessary risks where my freedom's concerned. And it's Friday now. So it's very urgent. It's as soon as possible. Like, perhaps we go to my office now and log on to your employer's database?" I was calm but insistent.

"It's late, Martin. But if it's really that important . . . ."

We were out of there inside three minutes. Kafka had to placate his 'acquaintances,' but I wasn't concerned with that. We went back through the rain. I unlocked my office and dug out my cocaine. I had been looking forward to it, but I passed it to Kafka without whimpering too much. While I started up the computer and got it connected I heard him hoovering it up. The computer did its thing and then we were up and running.

I told Kafka everything that I could remember about what the girl had told me in the Star. I told him about me and Karen. And about Barry. About the feeling I had that he was behind this. But how the hell could Barry frame me for murder?

Kafka sniffed deeply and sat down in front of the computer. He tapped at the keyboard.

"I'm in," he muttered. He fished around in his pocket for his notebook. "Right, what have we got? Archaeological digs. CCTV. I'll see what there is on the archaeological society . . . and Martin?"

"Huh?"

"What happened to your furniture?"

CHAPTER 6

VERY STRANGE

I woke up a couple hours later and stiffly lifted my head from the arm of the couch, grimacing with pain. A dull throbbing in my head was trying to annoy me. It was still dark outside. The desk light still cast its yellow pall over the room. I waited for the office to swim into focus, and saw that Kafka was gone. There were a couple of A4 printouts in front of me. No synapses were firing in my brain, so I hobbled across and made myself an instant coffee.

I flicked a glance at the papers. Lots of writing. I slurped at my coffee. It was horrible. But I drank it. You'd have drunk it, too. This wasn't the time for worrying about it.

OK MARTIN, HERE'S WHAT I COULD FIND SO FAR. IF I FIND ANY MORE I'LL PHONE YOU. IT'S ALL A BIT WEIRD. NOT WHAT I EXPECTED. CALL ME AND TELL ME AGAIN WHAT EXACTLY HAS HAPPENED SO FAR. K.

Weird? I didn't like the sound of that. I didn't like the word. I could think of a few words I'd have preferred. Like 'okay.' Or 'don't worry.' My watch said 4:30 A.M. That didn't look too nice either. I'd been half hoping that this whole stupid business was going to have disappeared. That I'd been hallucinating or something. Having a nightmare. But no. I lit a cigarette and started reading.

Charlcombe Archaeological Dig.
Work contracted out by archaeological society and the area council. The society and the council have effectively no control over the dig and expect only to be served with resulting data and any significant finds. Contract awarded to Kelley Historical Services. KHS have no website and are not listed at Companies House. KHS also awarded contract for a dig at the Circus in 1993. Data from that one is unavailable and there were 'no significant finds.' Other archaeological work contracted out to KHS consists of what's termed a 'minor' dig at lod gate (?), this latter completed in 2000. Again there was no data available from the database. Significant finds include Roman 'curse tablets,' partial Roman, Saxon, medieval, and more modern skeletons. The skeletons were found in different segments in different areas but were discovered to belong to only nine individuals. The most recent skeleton was dated at approximately 1900. They also found the remains of some elaborate saws of some kind, presumed to have a ceremonial function. This doesn't sound much like a 'minor' dig to me. The only current excavation is at Charlcombe, where the stated objective is 'continued research into Roman activity in the area.' The work there commenced six weeks ago and is due to run another two weeks, after which the site will be restored to its previous use, which was farmland. There is no data for this dig, and as yet 'no significant finds' according to the sources I searched.
CCTV in the city has been run previously by a number of commercial concerns including Rentokil(!). It is now run

by ScryTech, who describe themselves as 'a data gathering service.' They have a website which looks very cheap and contains no information of interest. I did find them in the Companies House database, but it was one of the most elusive entries I've ever seen. Again, their presence here is the result of a contract put out to tender by the area council. The most startling thing about their corporate objectives is that they aren't pushing for more cameras (i.e., more money) unlike their predecessors. Interestingly, ScryTech also provide CCTV security for KHS excavations.

I looked out of the window. I could see the rain running down the glass. I put the papers down on my desk, and had a little think about Karen Eliot. I wondered where she was. What she was doing. Sleeping, probably. Next to Barry, probably. I made another instant coffee and sat down again. 4:40 A.M. This was dead time. I started calculating the hours I had left. Christ. I still wasn't sure whether this was a setup, or what. This all seemed too . . . detailed for Barry. Too clever. Too deep. I remembered what the girl in the Star had said.

The head will be found on the east pediment. Staring up at the sky. The city will not shrug its shoulders. The city will demand a culprit. And you, Mister Valpolicella, will be the culprit.

Dismantled skeletons. Bodies. Nasty . . . very nasty . . . .

Okay. I picked up the sheets of paper again, even though I didn't want to. I really didn't want to.

I also dug up something else on KHS. They ended up being responsible for moving all materials from the old city library buildings to a new site. Initially was to be done in-house by the area council. Due to unspecified administrative problems, work was contracted out to an outfit named as Kelley Historical Services(!). This was put to the vote at a council meeting. According to the recorded minutes from the meeting, the motion was carried unanimously with one abstention from a B Eliot. There was and is no Eliot on the council so I don't know why his name is on the documentation.

The move from the old library to the new buildings was carried out with no problems. KHS were subsequently employed to control the new computer filing system for the library. Again, no apparent problems. At least none I could find out about. I'll see if I can do some more on this tomorrow.

Well, Martin. This all seems a little odd to me. I want to know how bad things are to make you want my help. Maybe I can help you some more. But I think you need to sleep. You really do look terrible. Call me in the morning.

K.

I glanced at my reflection in the rain-streaked window and knew that I needed more than a couple hours sleep to make me look any better. I needed a month of unconsciousness. Perhaps a couple of decades of cryogenic suspension would help. But somehow I doubted it. And anyway, it *was* the morning. Yeah, well. But too early to call Colin Kafka. Too early to call anyone who had any sense at all. But not too early to walk over to Charlcombe to see what might be what. To examine the work of Kelley Historical Services. Not too early. Not for me. I lit another cigarette, shoved the half-bottle of whiskey in my overcoat pocket, and slammed the door behind me.

CHAPTER 7

THINGS COULD ONLY GET WORSE

It was beginning to be what you might have called a beautiful summer morning. If it hadn't been raining. Mist shrouded the world, and maybe there was some kind of promise that the sun would be around later on. But maybe not. I walked up through a suburb, and as I left the city behind everything started getting beautiful on me, but I wasn't in the mood.

The grass was soaking wet and my breath hung in the air like a dead man. I'd fallen asleep in wet clothes and woken up to a horror story. I'd had almost no sleep and now I was in a sodden field at dawn. And I had a yawning suspicion that things could only get worse.

The Kelley Historical Services dig was at the top of the footpath, just below the church that lurked in a fold of the valley. Most of the excavations were under big blue tarpaulins stretched over a wooden framework of some kind. There was no one about, so I parted the strands of barbed wire and stepped through. I remembered what Colin had written about ScryTech's CCTV covering KHS digs.

I scanned the area under the tarp. There seemed to be three cameras, strategically placed for maximum coverage. I worked out a route that should keep me out of view. There was enough room to walk upright under the tarps, but only just. Under the tarp the mud looked blue, and my eyes took a while to adjust to the strange monochrome. There didn't seem to be much going on at the edges of the dig, so I walked on further. There were a lot of planks around, which I guessed were for walking on. None of the various trenches and holes held much interest for me. What did intrigue me was a very, very deep hole under the centre of the tarpaulin. Oh no. I was intrigued again. A bad sign.

It was bone dry under the centre of the tarp. The hole was what, seven or eight feet in diameter. And it was deep. It disappeared into inky darkness. I didn't care to think how deep it might be. Because I knew there was only one way that I could find out. There were props holding the sides steady. There was a winch built over the hole. There was a ladder. This was not an average archaeological dig that I was looking at. I remembered my watch and gave it a cursory inspection. 6 A.M.

On a regular archaeological dig no one should be here before 8:30. Especially on a Saturday. But, like I said, it was obvious that this wasn't a regular dig. It wasn't a regular anything. Hell, it wasn't a regular morning. I should have been in bed. So I had a drink of my whiskey. And I started climbing down the ladder.

It was colder as I went deeper, and there was a peculiar smell rising from the darkness below me. I was badly equipped for this sort of crap. No flashlight. No camera. No idea what the hell I was doing. I carried on climbing down into increasing darkness, foot after foot, hand after hand. Every time I looked up I saw a smaller circle of blue light above me. It was not a comfortable sight. A blue circle floating in a sea of black. I began to feel dizzy, as if the walls were constricting, and I was trapped in a vertical tube and there was nothing else in the world. Nothing else anywhere. Utterly alone. And the stench from beneath was stronger, an almost choking sulphurous stink.

I leant my head against a cold rung. I had to get to the bottom of this. As soon as the thought came into my mind I laughed aloud, and my laughter echoed hysterically around me until it slowly died out in what sounded like the mutterings of a devil. I took some deep breaths through my mouth. Step after step. Rung after rung. I had a nasty moment when the ladder seemed to disappear, but it was only where two ladders had been roped together somehow. I tried to empty my mind. Think about nice things. I thought about Karen Eliot naked in a bed, but then I started thinking about Barry and then about the Council and then about KHS and then I was back where I was. At the bottom of the hole. I was standing on stone. It was darker than any night. The blue circle that was my only visual connection to the surface seemed impossibly distant. I felt the cold floor beneath my feet. I felt around with my hands. Long cuts, or grooves, separated areas of flat stone. And then I realised. Flagstones. I was standing on a paved floor. Sixty feet or so beneath a rural valley in England.

I felt around the sides of the hole. It wasn't continuous. At times the walls just weren't there. My hands traced nothingness. There had to be tunnels, or at least deep hollows, radiating like spokes from the hole. All of them seemed to be paved, like the floor I was standing on. And no way was I crawling down them. Not now. Not without a light. No way. Not without several more stiff drinks inside me. I fumbled in my pocket and had another swig. Some cocaine would have been good. Lots of it. I suddenly got the fear. Badly.

I climbed back up the ladder, as fast as my cold arms and legs would take me. I seemed to move as slowly as a child hauling sacks of coal. The blue circle seemed to stay the same size for weeks, but eventually I could see the sides of the hole next to me, faintly illuminated by that eerie light. At long last I reached the surface. And I appreciated it. It's a fine place, the surface. I swore I'd never take it for granted again. I stumbled out, hoping that my erratic path would somehow avoid the cameras, and burst out into the open air like someone who's been underwater for almost too long. Almost long enough to drown.

It was still raining. The sun had obviously decided to spend the day somewhere else. I wished I had that choice. But I didn't. Choices were closing down around me like slamming doors. It was nearly 7:30 A.M. I walked back down towards the city as quickly as I could.

I had a flat on a street north of the city centre. It wasn't one of my favourite streets, but the rent was cheap. I let myself in. I showered and dumped my muddy, soaking clothes on the floor. I gave the flat a cursory glance. What a tip. I put on a suit, one of my less threadbare numbers. I had an idea, and I guessed that I needed to look at least semi-presentable for it to work. Then I called Kafka on his mobile.

"Who is this?" he asked. Just woken voice. Not too pleased. But I couldn't afford to worry about that. Things were getting too strange, too quickly.

"It's Martin. I need to meet you right now."

"Jesus. It's—what—eight-thirty on fucking Saturday morning." He muttered a few choice phrases then seemed to pull himself together. "Okay, okay . . . I'll see you at, oh, I dunno . . . ." He fumbled with words for a while, then mentioned a café. "You know it? I'll see you in, what, about half an hour. You're buying the coffee. Bye."

I strode briskly in the rain through town to where the café was. It was a fairly civilised place, but it was near the city Baths, and as I passed them I shuddered. *The head will be found on the east pediment. Staring up at the sky.* I thought of the hole at Charlcombe, the paved floor, and the tunnels. This morning, anything seemed possible. Murder, mutilation, my arrest—anything. Anything at all. Twenty-four hours and my world had been turned upside down. Back to front. Any which way but right.

CHAPTER 8

NO MESSAGES

I arrived at the café at the same time as Kafka, which I took to be
a good omen. I needed some good omens. We took a table at the
back of the café, ordered a couple of coffees.

He raised his eyebrows, lit a cigarette, and asked me to tell
him everything. I filled him in on what had happened since I last
saw him—I told him about Charlcombe. He was a good listener,
even though I didn't much like the expression that gathered force
on his face as I related my tale.

"It stinks, Martin. This whole thing reeks. KHS obviously
have an agenda that goes far beyond archaeological research. The
fact that they also control the city's library is suspicious, especially
when coupled with the fact that they suddenly acquired the
contract to move the books from the old site to the new one.
I don't like the '*no significant finds*' bit from the digs they've
already done either. It begins to seem like they're not after relics
at all. At least, not the kind of relics you'd expect."

I took a slurp of my coffee.

"I don't 'expect' any fucking kind of anything. Where do I fit
into this? Why am I being fed this information? I mean, they
practically drew me a map. I was expressly told to check out the
Charlcombe dig. Whoever is doing this knows all the answers

51

already. Why do I have to find them out all over again? And, more to the fucking point, why can't they leave me the hell out of it?" I said wearily.

"I'm not sure, but it could be that someone in KHS has broken ranks. They're too scared—of something—to do anything about it themselves so they've picked you to do their work for them. Maybe the bit about you getting arrested is just to get you sufficiently self-interested to basically do their bidding. Maybe the arrest—your arrest—is a lie." Kafka raised his eyebrows.

"I like that idea. I like it a lot," I growled.

"Who was the woman you met with at the Star?"

"She didn't say. I asked. She didn't tell. I asked her about Eliot—Barry Eliot—but she didn't seem to know who he was. As far as I could tell."

"Okay, but his is the only name we have. And you say that he knows that you've been—sleeping—with his wife. Interesting. What does he do for a living?"

"He's a property developer. A bigshot. He's connected with most of the grandest projects around here. He's—fuck, he's connected with everything important. Shit. I bet he's been involved with all the sites that KHS have worked on, before the building started. And I've been sleeping with his wife." I sat back in my chair and exhaled deeply. Something was adding up to something. The trouble was I had very little idea what any of the somethings were. All I knew was that I didn't like any of them.

"So." Kafka was pensive. His mouth twisted. "So. This Barry Eliot guy is connected—somehow or other—with KHS. Someone has been spoon-feeding you information about KHS. They've threatened you with the possibility of arrest—for murder. They've described a murder scene that is connected with a heritage site. The body is supposed to be discovered on the morning of the 13th July. Your arrest is supposed to be scheduled for that afternoon. They've even given the arrest a time of day, which is, on the face of it, unbelievable. KHS seem to work almost exclusively with heritage sites, and with libraries or books. What's going on?"

Questions were coming thick and fast. Answers weren't in the building.

"I'm getting more interested in this ScryTech outfit," I said. "I saw their cameras at the Charlcombe site. I'm pretty sure I avoided them though. ScryTech are in deep with KHS. Now, Colin, I had a little idea that I could check them out. Go see them. As a journalist doing a story. A little piece for your newspaper. A puff job. How CCTV cuts street crime, that kind of shit. Obviously I'll need a press pass. And I'll need the interview to be booked from a phone line in your offices. I know that it's a Saturday. Make something up about overtime."

"What?" He suddenly looked unhappy. I didn't care.

"Come on, Colin. You can do it."

Kafka squirmed. "I suppose you're right. I'll arrange an interview and call you to tell you when it will be. I'll lend— lend—you my press pass so you can copy it. Put . . . er . . . 'Bob Jones' on it. I'll find out what I can about Barry Eliot. But listen. I do not, repeat not—want my job fucked up in any way whatsoever."

"When have I ever fucked anything up?" I asked, pulling on my 'I'm hurt' face. Kafka just stared back at me. He dug in his pocket and flicked me his press pass. He got up.

"I'll call you," he said, and walked out into the rain. I stared blankly into space for a couple of minutes, and then I left, too.

I let myself into the office and checked my answerphone. More out of habit than anything else. It beeped and robot-voiced away while I poured a smallish whiskey and sat down. No messages. That was good. I lit a cigarette. The rain splattered against the window with a force that seemed close to anger. No messages, huh? I felt a small relief. So, I had a little time to think. Well. Okay. My plan was to get into the ScryTech CCTV control room. The city had plenty of their cameras around, swivelling and tracking events on the streets below. The idea was that the cameras deterred or prevented crime. The practical reality, I suspected, was entirely different. There had to be a reason why ScryTech and KHS had taken over significant chunks of the Area Council's operations at roughly the same time. ScryTech's stated job description was 'data gathering.' Surveillance. Watching, recording. KHS's purpose was digging, excavating, revealing. The library was, I reasoned, a repository of data. Somewhere in this maze there was a centre, an objective. A purpose.

Something told me that whoever was behind all of this hadn't got what it was that they wanted. Or maybe they had. Maybe they had what they wanted, had it all along. But I was being thrust into events, for a reason that remained obscure. I had a hunch that, despite what I had said to Colin Kafka, I was about to fuck things up. And it wasn't my fault. Honestly. Swearing under my breath, I pulled Kafka's press pass from my inside pocket and set about duplicating it. It wasn't hard. It didn't need to be a perfect copy. I was only going to flash it and slide it back in my wallet.

Kafka's call came at 10:40 A.M. I was ready. I'd already burnt a book of matches one by one, made lots of holes in a piece of A4 with the hole punch, and stared with blank eyes at the rain for a while.

"Martin? Have you done the press card?" Kafka sounded busy. Efficient. I grunted affirmatively. "Good. They'll want ID. I've set up an interview for 'Bob Jones' at eleven thirty this morning. You've got half an hour because crime fighting is, as we all know, a full-time job. Don't ask wrong questions. Okay?"

"I'm indebted, Colin," I spat. "What, exactly, constitutes a 'wrong' question? Don't tell me. I know. One that might get you into trouble. Well, don't worry. You know me. But yeah, well, thanks. So where do I go to meet with ScryTech? And should I let you know what gives?"

"Do that, Martin. I'm hoping to get some sort of story out of this. Assuming you don't upset too many people. You'll meet a Council official called Mario Murnau in the lobby of City Hall." He hung up.

CHAPTER 9

WET HANDSHAKE

I was punctual. I always am. My suit was still looking reasonably sharp, despite the drizzle I arrived in. I climbed the steps up to City Hall and pushed open the double doors. The lobby was spacious, all marble and Victorian civic ostentation. There was a secretary behind a lonely desk that looked tiny and out of place in the chilly vastness.

"My name's Bob Jones. From the paper. I'm supposed to be meeting Mario Murnau," I said. I hoped I sounded polite. I couldn't tell. Well, yeah.

"I'll just page him. Is he expecting you?" Icy cold. Professional, I supposed. But not very welcoming. Well, yeah. What did I expect? Air kisses and a hug?

"I have an appointment for eleven thirty."

"Well, it's only eleven twenty-five. Would you take a seat?"

I bit back a few choice words and sat down. I sat still and I looked around until I'd looked around about as much as I cared to. It wasn't very rewarding. Murnau turned up a quarter of an hour later. I got up and extended my hand, but he didn't seem to like the idea of shaking it. He walked towards the door. I followed.

"Bob Jones? I'm Murnau. I take it you're here to talk to the CCTV chappies." Mario Murnau was tall, with horn-rimmed specs, and a polished, vaguely Etonian accent. His name sounded exotic, but he didn't look it. There was something a little odd about him, though. I couldn't quite tell what it was. We were outside now. The rain didn't surprise me. I was used to it. Murnau didn't like it at all. He hurriedly unlocked a black wrought-iron gate, and led me down some steps below the pavement. I'd never noticed them before.

"They live down here, Bob. The men behind our electronic eyes! Night and day, twenty-four hours, they never stop. Shifts, of course. Ah, could I just see your press card? Good, good. Have to be careful, you realise. Where was I? Yes, indeed, the system is never unattended. Never! Round the clock safety and peace of mind for the good citizens of our city, eh? Anyway, it's all pretty sensitive stuff, so I'll stay with you while you speak to the chappies. Don't mind me."

We had entered a subterranean control room beneath City Hall. It seemed unnecessarily dark. There were banks of switches and two walls of TV monitors, both colour and black and white. Figures moved across them. I could recognise most of the locations. There was a reek of body odour and instant coffee in the stuffy atmosphere. Murnau took a couple of steps back into the murk of the corner of the room. He was proprietorial. Watchful. And not entirely at ease. There were three men scrutinising the screens, their faces lit up by them. One of them, a bulky crew-cut guy in some sort of pseudo military pullover, turned on his swivel chair and extended a meaty hand towards me.

"Morning. I'm Robinson. I take it you'd like to know a little about the system?" Robinson. No first name. He seemed friendly though. Almost keen. Probably welcomed the chance to see someone from outside. A reporter, no less.

"Bob Jones." I shook his hand. His handshake was moist. Not too firm. I didn't like it. Handshakes are one of the things that I tend to judge people on. Not fair, I know. Yeah, well. Anyway.

"I'm from the paper. I'm working on a piece about twenty-first century crime and prevention. Credit card fraud, Internet scams, that sort of thing. Then moving on to DNA testing, 'smart water,' and of course video surveillance. Which is where you guys come in. All right to smoke in here?" I had my cigarette already in my mouth.

"I'm afraid not, Bob," said Murnau. I put my cigarette back in the packet.

"Well," said Robinson, "basically, we inherited this system from Rentokil. The Council reviews the contract every three years. If everything's up to scratch, nothing changes. Or if another company offers a better deal than the current outfit, that's taken into consideration at the review. So we have to perform!" He laughed. Murnau laughed, too. Stage laughter, I thought. "We have a total of a hundred and two cameras in the central city area, and thirty-six in the suburbs, another thirty-six in local villages—"

"Excuse me," I interrupted, pulling a notebook from my bag. "This is exactly the kind of thing we need our readers to know. Peace of mind, and all that." I scribbled down the figures.

"—so we have a total of one hundred seventy-four cameras operating in public areas. All of these cameras are highly visible. That's a requirement in the guidelines. No hidden cameras. Part of the point of them is to deter crime, as well as detect it. So visible cameras are part of the plot. Your criminal sees the camera and thinks again. Your criminal knows he's being watched. The knowledge that the cameras exist is enough to deter crime, at least in the first instance. Another part of the plot is that we don't want the surveillance to be seen as a covert, Big Brother–style operation. The cameras are friends to the law-abiding. It's your criminals who need to worry about them."

He laughed again. He was an irritating guy, self-satisfied and smug. With a wet handshake. I carried on scribbling in my notebook. I noticed Murnau straining to read what I was writing without seeming to.

"One of the cameras' sidelines is that they look out for each other, too. Each camera is sited so that I can check the status of its neighbouring device."

I was beginning to feel bored. I let the lecture drift on, occasionally nodding or making an appreciative noise. I kept on writing in my book. I knew all this anyway. Standard surveillance industry crap. Everything was smothered in layers of assurance that it was all for the public good. Old-fashioned crime-fighting Dixon-of-Dock-Green sweet-talk. I thought I might as well throw a small spanner into his spiel. Test out a little suspicion of mine.

"So how much money does KHS earn from the contract?" I asked.

"I'm afraid that information is classified," butted in Murnau. He looked at me sharply. "Standard business practice, of course. A company is under no obligation to reveal its finances to anyone other than the Inland Revenue."

"Of course," I concurred. Interesting. Murnau had responded quickly, but perhaps too quickly to notice exactly what I had said.

"Well, that's the background. Anything specific you'd like to ask?" said Robinson.

"That seems to have covered almost everything I need for the article. But I would like to see the cameras in action from here. Would that be possible?"

"Certainly. Take a seat." Robinson got up, while Murnau shifted, uncomfortably I thought, from foot to foot in the shadows. "Now, just take a look at that monitor there. General view down this street, one of our prime retail areas. Okay. Let's just zoom in . . . ." The view on the monitor barrelled down the street, to focus with astonishing clarity on a man standing at a junction at the end.

"That's incredible," I said. I meant it. Apart from the fact that for once it wasn't raining. The camera had zoomed in on a face maybe two hundred and fifty metres away. You could see the guy's moustache. His glasses. You could practically tell how long ago he'd shaved his chin.

"And watch *this*," gushed Robinson. He was proud of the hardware. "I'll just take a still . . . ." There was an audible click from somewhere inside the control desk, and the image froze. "Now what we can do is check this bloke's face on our database . . . ." Faces scrolled down the screen impossibly fast, dozens and dozens of them. Hundreds. Thousands. In just a few seconds the original still returned with the words NO MATCH emblazoned over it. "So there you have it. Visual mapping. His face has just been compared to all the criminals—convicted or otherwise—in our system archives. He's clear. No record. Well, not as far as we know. But if we have any reason to be suspicious, we can e-mail his mugshot to the central police archives, and they'll do a nationwide search. There's no hiding place for crooks in our city."

I was absolutely horrified.

"That's quite something," I said. "Very impressive. No hiding place for crooks in our city, hey? Might make a decent headline." Robinson glowed with pride. "Would it be all right to have a photographer come down, take a few pictures of you guys at work, in front of all the monitors?" I pretty much knew this would be refused, but I liked to tease. Robinson was thinking he was going to be famous. Of course, Murnau put the cosh on the notion immediately.

"I'm afraid that won't be possible, Bob," he interjected firmly from the gloom behind us. "We cannot put our chappies at risk from criminals who may have been convicted on the strength of video evidence. No, photography is completely out of the question. And no names must be used in your piece. We will naturally need to check it over before publication."

Robinson looked a little downcast. He was going to have to wait a while longer for his fifteen minutes of fame. I smiled inwardly. It was fine for these legitimised voyeurs to film, photograph, and file unknowing Joe and Jane Publics. But not okay for the process to be reversed. Yeah, well.

"What a shame. A photo's always nice to accompany blocks of text. But never mind. There's a couple of things I'd like to know, just to wrap things up. Do you have a map—a plan—of the areas covered by the cameras that I could look at? We will need some sort of graphic, if a photo's not possible. And do you have any plans to extend the network?"

"I can get you a map. One moment. And no, there are no plans to extend the network at present." Robinson was terse. Back to anonymity for you, friend. Being an unknown's not so bad though. And it looked from the technology in the room that anonymity was getting to be a rare thing. Getting rarer every day. A machine across the way, where Murnau was standing, purred quietly for a few seconds, then I was passed an A4 sheet.

"I'll show you out," said Murnau briskly. I'd had my allotted thirty minutes. I said my goodbyes to the 'chappies' and followed Murnau back up the steps, glad to breathe fresh air, if not so pleased to feel the rain on my face.

"Bloody weather," muttered Murnau under his breath.

"Must be quite a strange occupation," I said. "Watching telly all day in a basement."

"ScryTech do a very good job indeed. You'd be very surprised what we see." A policeman passed us on the steps. Murnau nodded curtly to him.

"Well, thanks very much for your time," I smiled. "It's been *very* interesting."

"Not a problem. Always happy to talk to our illustrious local newspaper. When will your piece appear? I expect Robinson would like to see it."

I bet he would, I thought.

"Oh, some time soon. Next week or so," I answered breezily. Don't hold your breath, Murnau. Don't wait up, Robinson.

"Goodbye then, Bob."

"Bye."

CHAPTER 10

SHINY NEW SHOES

It was just after midday. Town was packed. Shoppers and tourists everywhere, despite the rain and the wind. I glanced up. A black CCTV camera swivelled idly towards me, twenty feet above the crowds. Here's to you, Mister Robinson, I thought. I barged through the hordes back towards my office. I was definitely interested in the fact that Mario Murnau hadn't noticed my use of 'KHS' instead of 'ScryTech' when I'd asked him about the financing. Maybe I was even intrigued. A little idea about the relationship between KHS and ScryTech had germinated, and now it was growing fast. Like a fungus.

Another interesting thing was happening. I had a peculiar feeling that I was being watched. Not surprising, after 'interviewing' a surveillance company. Okay. But it was a more visceral feeling than that. An animal sense. It started as something vague, like a forgotten errand. But by the time I was halfway down the street that led to my office it had coalesced into a certainty. I was being followed. I stopped and inspected the windows of a bike shop. I wasn't going to do anything as stupid as look back. But I considered my options. If I went to my office now . . . . No. I wanted to stay on top of this. Hell, I needed to stay on top. Time was running out.

I darted across the road, through the usual slow-moving Saturday traffic jam. Making a bit more of car-avoiding than was really necessary, I ducked into a pub and shook the water off. I stood just inside the door and waited. My tail was just under one minute behind me. Smartly dressed. Pretty expensive clothes, and formal enough to look just a little out of place in this particular pub on a Saturday. He was a very big man, I thought. I'd turned to the bar, waiting to get served. He scanned the pub, quickly and efficiently. Okay. I wasn't trying to hide. I was just an honest journalist, having a drink after a bit of weekend work. Fair enough? Bet your life. I was covered. And very glad I hadn't gone straight back to the office, past the brass plaque by the door. That might have been something of a giveaway.

I got a pint and moved away from the bar, taking care to appear not to notice my unwelcome companion. He checked me out, seemed to come to the conclusion I was legit. He did some kind of 'my friend isn't here after all' mime and left. I found a seat and pulled out my cigarettes. I'd been a convincing reporter, I thought. I'd had a press pass. I'd been fairly predictable. A bit stupid. I didn't think I'd asked any of those 'wrong' questions that Colin had been so keen for me to avoid. Why had the Council, or, more likely, ScryTech/KHS thought it necessary to have me tailed?

I finished my pint. Scurried out into the rain after checking there was no nosey smart dressed man hanging around. I'd gone fifteen yards when a car pulled up next to me. Expensive. Shiny. The tinted passenger window rolled down electrically and a voice said, "Get in."

I leant down to look in at the speaker, but before I could open my mouth, one of the back doors opened, someone from behind manhandled me into the back seat, shoved themselves in after me and there I was, sandwiched between two huge guys. It was like the one who'd tailed me had a twin or something. It was expertly done, and I fought back a scream as it happened. The car started moving immediately, and we were heading out of the city before I could speak.

"What the fuck is this?" I spluttered.

"Be quiet. Do not speak until you're asked to," said the guy in the passenger seat. He had a very even voice. No emotion at all. He didn't turn round. Everyone in the car was looking straight ahead. They wore dark clothes, not suits, but pretty smart all the same. What was this type of clothing called? Oh yeah, 'smart casual.' Everything looked new. And very, very normal. Very respectable. The car, their clothes, everything. There wasn't even any scuffing on the shoes of the two apes I was squashed between. I considered my options. There didn't seem to be any. So I considered them again. Still nothing.

"You ask the questions, right?" I said. A huge elbow drove into my stomach and I shut up very fast. I was too busy gasping. Tears squeezed up behind my eyes. We were out on the main road heading north, moving fast, when I got my breath back. Nobody spoke. We pulled off the road in a lay-by next to the junction with the motorway. One of the gorillas opened his door and I was persuaded with little difficulty to get out with them. The passenger door opened and the only one who'd spoken got out, too. He was quite a little guy. He put up an umbrella. He looked straight into my eyes.

"What is your name?" His voice was curt, and still showed no emotion at all. He sounded like an automaton. I wondered what to say.

"Bob Jones."

He seemed to consider this for a minute.

"Who are you working for?"

"I'm a journalist. I work for the local paper. Want to see my press card?" He nodded. Well, he moved his head slightly.

I reached slowly into my pocket and got my forgery. I wished I'd spent a little more time on it. The little guy took it and examined it. Then he passed it in to the driver.

"Check this name," he said. And we stood there in silence, cars rushing past us on their way to somewhere else. Rain was running down my forehead into my eyes, but the gorillas held my arms at my sides so there wasn't anything I could do about it. A couple of minutes went by, not as quickly as I'd have liked. Then a hand emerged from the driver's window, holding my card.

"There is no record of any 'Bob Jones' working for any newspaper within two hundred miles," said the driver's voice. "And this card is fake. Not even a good fake."

Oh, shit. The little guy's eyes left mine for an instant while he glanced at both the gorillas. Then I was marched through a gate into a field, and flung into the soaking wet grass. They didn't give me a chance to get up. A heavy foot encased in a shiny shoe stood on each of my upper arms and it wasn't too nice being face down either.

"Who are you working for?" said the little guy again.

"I don't know," I shouted into the grass. "I'm being fucked about and I don't know what's going on and can I please get up *for fuck's sake?*"

The shoes got off my arms and one of them rolled me over. Rain poured into my face.

"Look, I'm being set up by someone. I don't know who or why. I'm trying to find out what's going on." I tried to get up, but I was pushed back onto the ground.

"Mister Jones, if that is indeed your name," said the little guy, "if you have any interest in living a comfortable life I suggest you stop trying to find out, as you say, what's going on. Cease your puerile enquiries." He said the words with disgust, as if he was talking about sewage. I sat up, cautiously. I'd been wetter and more uncomfortable before. When I'd drunkenly stumbled into a canal one February night. But I had to admit it. This was pretty bad.

"Do I have your agreement?" It was less a question, more a statement. I reckoned the easiest course of action was to nod. I nodded. He stared shrewdly at me, then turned back towards the car. I looked at the gorillas, and tried to get up again. No dice. Those shiny new shoes had other ideas.

CHAPTER 11

VERY LARGE DRINK

I lay there in the rain for quite a while, groaning and stuff. An expert kicking had been delivered, and I couldn't fault the twins' technique. They hadn't said a word. They hadn't grunted, hadn't got out of breath, and they hadn't even laughed as they walked back to the car after an action-packed three minutes. Okay. I watched raindrops trickling down the broken stems of the grass and wondered what to do. If they'd wanted to hurt me really badly, then they could have. As it was, parts of me hurt, but nothing was too badly damaged. Nothing broken. It had been a warning.

Delicately I eased myself into a standing position. Parts of me definitely hurt. But I could walk. I made my way out of the field. The lay-by was empty. Yeah, well. Wearily I trudged to the edge of the road and stood with my back to the city for a time. I had nowhere else to go, so I faced the oncoming traffic and stuck my thumb out. I wasn't an ideal hitcher. I was wet through, muddy, and didn't look very happy.

After about three centuries a pickup truck slowed to a halt. I ran to catch up with it, stated my destination, and made to get in the passenger seat. The driver, a squat sort of guy with a checked shirt and a strong smell of engine oil about him, pointed at my clothes and shook his head. I climbed into the back of the truck, ready to enjoy some more weather.

And me in my best suit, I said to myself. The truck got me back to town, more or less. Okay. I had to get back to my flat. I couldn't do anything in this state. I needed a shower, new clothes, and perhaps something to eat. Scratch that. I needed a very large drink. The walk back up to the flat was pretty much unremitting agony, but I got home in the end. My place was still a tip, but in a sort of comforting way. It wasn't unexpected, intriguing, or interesting. It didn't ask me impossible questions or beat me up in remote fields. And for that I was deeply grateful.

CHAPTER 12

SERIOUSLY BAD NEWS

By the time I felt okay it was nearly 6 P.M. The flat was okay, but it wasn't any kind of place to think. That was one of the reasons why I had an office. And that's where I went. I'd learnt one thing from the little guy with the emotionless voice and the big friends. So I dug out an umbrella. I bought some supplies on the way—whiskey, cigarettes, and I nipped in to the house of a guy I knew and picked up some cocaine.

I had a feeling that I might be needing it. But I only had time to do about five minutes' thinking when I got down to the office, because the thought I had after five minutes was that I was supposed to meet the famous Stonehenge T-shirt at 7 P.M., which was now about a quarter of an hour away. Okay. I looked at my furniture. I had a quick whiskey and locked the office again.

Saturday night is not a calm night anywhere in the world. So I was expecting it to be busy, even early in the evening, but it seemed to be pretty mellow in the Old Green Tree. There were a few old colonel types drinking in the public bar, and a couple talking quietly in the lounge. That was it. No Stonehenge T-shirt. I ordered a pint of lager and sat down in the lounge, trying not to overhear what the couple were talking about. Sounded pretty interesting until I realised they were discussing *EastEnders*.

I lit a cigarette and stared at the wall. And I carried on with the thinking I'd been intending to do. Okay. ScryTech and KHS were one and the same thing, I figured. Barry Eliot had something to do with it all, but I couldn't tell what. The Charlcombe dig was not about archaeology, at least not in any normal sense. KHS were obviously withholding data and hiding finds. Okay. I decided that firstly I was going to call Karen Eliot and get her to tell me all about Barry. And I was going to go back up to Charlcombe with a flashlight, a camera, a fresh half-bottle of whiskey, and my wrap of Charlie.

I was going to check out those tunnels. I guessed that Saturday night was a good time to do it. Those 'archaeologists' would probably be far away, down the pub somewhere. The warning delivered by the smartly dressed bastards with their fucking shiny shoes was not an issue. So—I was fucked if I did anything. But the same applied if I didn't.

I'd just got my mobile out to call Karen when a big fat guy wearing a beard and a slightly stained Stonehenge T-shirt came in. He went up to the bar and I heard him order a pint. Real ale. That figures, I thought. Then he turned around and walked straight towards me, pulled out the chair opposite, and sat down. He took a massive swig of his ale. Without looking at me he took out a packet of tobacco and made a rollup. He lit it with a battered Zippo, took a huge drag, and exhaled the smoke in my face. Then his eyes met mine.

I sighed, ran my hands over my face, and said, "Panto. Very nice. Why an Ugly Sister though? You'd make a great Cinderella."

He narrowed his eyes. "Hmm. For someone in as much trouble as you are, you've still got a sense of humour. Look after it. You might not have much else after Monday."

"Look," I said. "I'm very tired. I've been very busy. And it hasn't been easy. Some big men have been nasty to me. Almost everyone else has been elusive, insulting, and generally difficult. And it never stops fucking raining. So, listen . . . I'd really, really appreciate it if you just state your business, tell me whatever it is you're here to tell me, and then leave me the fuck alone. Is that too much to ask?"

"You been up to Charlcombe yet? Have you any idea what's going down?"

"I've been up. I've been down. I've been all over. You know what?" I was suddenly very bored. "You know what? If the next sentence you utter doesn't grab me, I'm gone. As of that moment. I'm gone. Are you hearing me? Catching my drift?" I lit another cigarette and closed my eyes for a couple of heartbeats.

"Hey." He looked a little perplexed. With that I could identify. "Calm down. I'm here to help you. Help you. Understand?"

As you can imagine, I'd had enough help to last me a long time. None of it did the job though. None of it helped. All it did was get me deeper into something I had no wish to even dip my toes in. "Okay," I said. "Help me then. Yes, I've been up to Charlcombe. They've got a big hole there. It goes a long way in a direction I don't like. Who, exactly, are you?"

"Think of me as your friend. My name's not necessary for you to know. I've got some information for you. *Now, do you want it?*"

I sighed, again. I ran my hands over my face, again. "Yes," I said, exhaling.

I stared at my empty glass for a little while, realised he wasn't going to offer to get it filled up again, excused myself, bought another pint, and sat down again.

"Look," I said patiently. Well, yeah. Impatiently. "Before you begin, just by sitting here with you I'm implicating myself in this further and further."

Maybe I should have just ignored the note, the e-mail, I thought. I shouldn't have gone to see that woman in the Star.

I shouldn't have gone to the dig at Charlcombe. I should have avoided the CCTV place like the plague. But I didn't. I went and got all intrigued about it. Then I got myself a kicking in a farmer's field next to the motorway. I sighed again. The practice was improving my delivery.

"Okay," I muttered, lighting another cigarette, "tell me what you know."

"Listen. There's something under the city. It's been there a very long time, since, well, maybe forever. A darkness. But it's a darkness people have been using, or trying to use, for, well, a long time. Thing is, now they've worked out how to use it. For real. And that? That is seriously bad news."

"Whoa there. Two things. Who are 'they'? What is 'it'?" I interrupted.

"*They* are . . . they are kind of—the elite. I'm not talking about the old 'Establishment' here, not the Bilderbergers, not the oligarchs. They are just . . . dilettantes, compared to this lot. No one name describes them or does them justice. They are the folks who *really* run things. The top dogs. They are very powerful people who can never get too much power. They call themselves AFFA. In their own tongue, in a language from a very long time back, AFFA means 'nothing.' It isn't an acronym for anything. It is—just a word. If you call yourself nothing, no one knows who you are. Or what you want.

"They—AFFA—always want more. And now—right now— They have the means to change the world. I want you to think about what I'm saying. Power has always been fought for. Next king, next queen, next pope, president, whatever. It's a fight, a very, very dirty fight. *Power, by any means necessary.* These people are above morals. Morals are there to keep the likes of us in line. But They, the elite, AFFA, will do anything at all to get and keep power. And now, after centuries of work, the ultimate power, the absolute power to do exactly as they please is finally within Their grasp."

"I know all about this," I said, "because I watch *The X-Files*. Next. Next please. What is 'it'?"

The man sighed. Nice. His turn. I felt better all of a sudden. "It has had many names. None of them do it justice. I guess you've heard of alchemy, of the Philosopher's Stone, through your avid TV watching? The Philosopher's Stone is an agent of transmutation. To turn lead into gold—that was the stated goal of the alchemists. But physical transmutation is a metaphor. Alchemy—the use of the Philosopher's Stone—is actually about controlling *everything*. It's about controlling the *world*."

What a fucking joker. He sounded like some kind of zealot. Or something. I didn't trust him to the end of my pint.

"You said that your name isn't important. Maybe it isn't. So don't tell me. But tell me why I should even waste my time shooting the breeze with you. Because you're sure as hell not whoever you're pretending to be."

He glared at me for a little while before he answered.

"I will," he said in a low voice, "after you tell me what you know so far. Tell me your thoughts. Tell me what you've found out."

"Why the hell should I tell you? I've done the hard work so far, in my opinion. Finding stuff out, climbing down holes. I got abducted. I got a kicking. By fucking Tweedledum and fucking Tweedledee. Not you, mister whoever you are. It hurt a lot. Why should I tell you anything at all?"

He grinned. It wasn't a smile. I got to see a lot of his teeth.

"What else are you going to do with what you know? With what you have? What else can you do but tell someone who might believe you? Who else can you tell?"

He had something there. What was I going to do next? I was sunk badly into a situation that I seemed to have less control over with every hour that passed. He was right, really. Who else could I tell? Here was mister Stonehenge T-shirt, right in front of me. He was part of this, whatever it was. Not for the first time, I took a look at my options and felt the usual growing dismay. All of this buzzed around my brain for, well, about three seconds. I put on a pensive, intelligent expression for another minute or so, just to save face.

"You're right, I guess," I said. It wasn't a thing I said often, and my voice caught a little as the words came out. Lack of practice.

"So?" he asked. I took a deep breath or two and told him. About what had happened so far. About my suspicions about KHS and ScryTech. About the deep hole at Charlcombe. About the slight strangeness of my 'interview' with the CCTV operatives and Murnau. About being followed, and gave a vehemently described account of my time both in and outside of the shiny, expensive car. Then I asked him, also pretty vehemently, who the fuck he was. I think I asked him to tell me without delay. Something like that.

"I'm an academic. I was asked by a close friend to speak to you. I must apologise for the subterfuge. We needed to know if you were as reliable as we'd hoped you'd be. You should also know, by the way, that the woman you met last night in the Star was an actor, a former student of mine . . . . Now then, we are very concerned about what is happening. Very concerned. And I'm sorry about the violence you suffered today. Their security is even tighter than we imagined."

"We? They? I guess 'they' are 'them.' AFFA. Who are you calling 'we'?"

"Perhaps we shouldn't talk here. Perhaps your office might be less . . . public?"

"Okay," I said, "but one thing before we go. I came in here last night and made some enquiries about you. I spoke to a barman. He's not here tonight. But he didn't seem to like you too well. Any ideas why that should be?"

"Tall fellow? Dark hair? Eyebrow piercing?"

I nodded. The guy grinned again. Teeth again. "Monty Cantsin. One of my students last year. He was hoping for a First. He got a Third, and he wasn't very happy about it."

I nodded, slowly. It sounded just about believable. Not much else did. I finished my pint and lit a cigarette. I nodded towards the door.

"Okay. Let's go to my office."

CHAPTER 13

BIOLOGICAL WEAPON

We didn't speak on the way. It was getting dark too early because of the rain. The street was crowded with people. Most of them had the weekend glint in their eyes. Alcohol, and lots of it, was on their agenda. Then sex or violence or some drunken species of misery. I kind of envied them. Even their misery would most likely be gone by the morning. Mine had legs though. Stamina. And it just kept on getting more nourishment.

We sidestepped the puddled vomit in the alley and I let us into the office. There was a message on the phone from Colin Kafka, asking me to call him urgently. Yeah, well. There's urgent and there's urgent. My main urgency was to find out what Stonehenge had to say. I checked the time. 9 P.M. Already. Something about the day was nagging at my mind. It was the guys in the car, mainly. I'd been followed, shoved into a car and driven out of town and interrogated, sort of. But would they have done that to just anyone? What if I'd been legit? Polite apologies and a lift back into town? Somehow it didn't quite gel. No, it didn't gel at all. They must have known very quickly that I wasn't who I said I was. That visual mapping thing . . . .

I remembered the CCTV camera I had looked up at after leaving the control room. If they had doubts about me, they

81

could have taken a zoomed-in still of my face, run it through their database, and—what? What could they have seen that would make them want to warn me off the whole deal? Did they have me on file already from somewhere else? If so, then where from? Maybe the cameras at Charlcombe had got me. I couldn't be sure that I'd avoided them all, especially on the way out from under the tarpaulin. Unless there'd been cameras actually down the hole. Infrared cameras? But why? I was getting nowhere. I got out the whiskey and poured a couple of glasses. I turned to Stonehenge and passed him one. He was sitting on the couch. I grabbed my remaining chair, pulled it over, and sat down facing him.

"You were going to tell me. Who's 'we'?"

"This might come as something of a surprise."

"Oh, goody. I like surprises. I've had more than my share recently, and you know what? I'm getting to like them. Now. Who is 'we'?"

"Barry Eliot and myself. Barry is, or rather was, closely involved with Them. Almost one of Them, you could say. He became involved through his wife. Through Karen. Who I think you know. Rather closely, I fear."

He had been right about the surprise. Except it was more of a shock. A jaw-dropper. I stared at him. I was paralysed. But it wasn't very long before it stopped being paralysis and became potentially fatal for my only chair. I might have said, 'Excuse me,' before I hurled it across the room, but I probably didn't. I did some swearing and only just stopped myself from throwing my drink after the chair. Okay. I could probably speak now. I looked back at Stonehenge. He was watching me. Warily, I thought. Well, yeah.

"Barry Eliot?" My words were choked.

He nodded. "Barry Eliot."

"You're asking me to accept that you and *Barry Eliot* are the good guys? Barry threatened to kill me two weeks ago. He threatened to get my licence revoked. And he plays golf. These are not the actions of a good guy."

"He walked in on you having sex with his wife. What did you expect him to do? Pat you on the back? He doesn't care about you sleeping with Karen. He hates her. But he can't let her know that. His is the only direct contact we have with Them. I assure you, Barry's outburst was entirely for Karen Eliot's benefit."

"You're kidding me," I said, but somehow I felt he wasn't. He shook his head slowly.

"Karen Eliot is one of—*Them?*"

He nodded again. I went over and picked up by chair. It wasn't broken. Thankfully. I sat down again. I needed to. I drained my whiskey. I looked around, a little wildly I think. Stonehenge leant over and handed me his still untouched whiskey. I drank that, too.

"Karen Eliot is one of this elite? One of these—AFFA fuckers? Who are about to have this ultimate power, whatever the fuck that is? Okay. If I'm going to believe this—any of it—you're going to need to tell me more. A lot more." I lit a cigarette and got another whiskey, in what order I don't remember. I don't expect you'd remember either, at a time like that.

"Yes. Karen Eliot isn't who you may have thought she was. She is one of a central core, or cabal, of twenty-three individuals concerned with—er, conducting business—under the city. What else would you like to know?"

"Okay. Okay." I thought for a minute. "*Under* the city? You said something about that before, in the pub. What is it? What is under the city?"

"Tunnels. Caverns. Labyrinths. They're very, very old. Some of them predate the Romans. A lot are medieval. Some are more modern. They are not widely known of, for the good reason that They keep it that way. Every drainage system, every pipeline laid, every new building . . . everything, anything, that disturbs the surface, is vetted exhaustively to ensure that there is no chance it will impinge on the tunnel system. The tunnels themselves are extensive. We don't know how far they extend, but the excavations being carried out by KHS at Charlcombe suggest that the network may run even as far as that."

"They do. At the bottom of that hole there were maybe three tunnels radiating off in different directions. It was all paved with flagstones or something. I couldn't easily tell. I didn't have my flashlight."

"Three tunnels? Interesting. There are probably the same number radiating from a cavern underneath the Circus."

"What the hell is it about the Circus? My contact tried to find out about the 1993 KHS dig there. He came up with zilch. 'No significant finds' or some such crap. And who the hell are KHS anyway?"

"All right. How can I explain this? The Circus is, well, is basically *Stonehenge*, rebuilt, *recreated*, in its perfect form." His eyes were gleaming.

I pointed to his T-shirt. "Hence the threads, eh?"

"Yes, hence the T-shirt. One of my particular specialities. Stonehenge itself is obviously badly dilapidated. The Circus is a much more modern temple, and it remains undamaged. Even after it was damaged in the Second World War it was perfectly repaired. Perfectly. Nowhere else in the entire country, in the whole of the UK, was repaired with such precision. The original architect himself was one of Them. He understood the power of the Neolithic temple at Stonehenge. He calculated the dimensions and placing of the stones as they were in the eighteenth century, and with the help of . . . certain . . . others extrapolated their data back through time. He finally came up with the right sums. He and his son designed both the Circus and the Royal Crescent, two of the more admired architectural creations in the entire country. Those two structures, combined with the streets between them, form a massive symbol on the face of the earth. It's generally given out that this represents the sun and the moon. It doesn't. It's AFFA's symbol. And it's as old as Stonehenge. Older. They had uncovered the matrix of Stonehenge as it was—how it was intended. Then they rebuilt it. They rebuilt it in here, in this city."

"All right. Okay. Just about. But why here?"

"Because here was—and is—their centre, their laboratory, or headquarters, or whatever. Their temple. The temple of AFFA. They have always been here. We don't know why. But this was the birthplace of alchemy. It may be that the hot water from the springs here was used in earlier experiments. Or in processes of some kind, or, well . . . I don't know. But the tunnels are the reason for it all. They're the key. They predate the Circus by centuries. *Centuries.* Possibly thousands of years. It was natural, deliberate, to build the temple here. Like your—er—contact, we haven't been able to find out much about the KHS dig there. But it's my guess that They're linking up lost parts of the subterranean system. Finding older, forgotten parts, and linking them. From what Barry has been able to find out from Karen, They're very close to completing the work."

I went over and picked up the bottle. I poured myself another, and took both the glass and the bottle back to my chair. I lit another cigarette, unsurprisingly.

"Mmm. How about that, then. Just how about that. This is about as weird as it gets, right? Anyway, I hope it doesn't get any weirder. Tunnels. I'd laugh in your face if I hadn't seen them—or sensed them—myself. Let's say I accept what you're telling me.

Okay. Two things. What's the score with Barry and Karen? And I asked you before, who are KHS?"

"Could I have a glass of that whiskey?"

"Sure." I poured.

"Karen Eliot is, as I said, one of Them. Barry didn't know this when he married her. He soon found out. Karen used him to, er, to supply sperm. Into specimen jars that were refrigerated and used, somehow, by Them. That is what Barry was for. That's what he had to do. In exchange, his property development firm became spectacularly powerful. He gained contacts, influential friends. He gained power. For a long time he was quite happy about the arrangement. But as he grew closer to Them, and was drawn into their circle of influence—well, then he began to feel scared. And he began to sense that he was witnessing the build-up—the rapid build-up—to something terrible. That was when he contacted me. My own studies include this, well, this sort of thing . . . he came across a paper of mine and thought that I might be able to help him find out what was going on and—if necessary—to stop it. Or try to."

"Sperm? For fuck's sake. This is ludicrous. And KHS? What's your explanation for them?"

"Kelley Historical Services is one of the organisations AFFA use to get things done in an apparently legitimate manner. KHS are named after Edward Kelley, who was alive in the sixteenth century. He was a medium. He could see, or at least talk to, spirits. Or angels. Whatever you like to call them. I would say that now the consensus is that they were—are—demons. He came here with his master, John Dee, Doctor John Dee. They travelled in great secrecy. There are virtually no records of their ever having visited, but it's more or less down to that pair that we are now facing the problems we are. They discovered, or were led by these demons to some alchemical materials that the prior of the Abbey had carefully hidden during the Dissolution of the Monasteries. These were very, very powerful materials. Very dangerous materials. I mean, a modern equivalent would be the *precisely labelled ingredients for a biological weapon.* That's how dangerous. And we think that these same materials are being used now. Today. By AFFA."

"Fucking hell. Okay. Right, I got to thinking that ScryTech were effectively the same outfit as KHS and, from what you say— Them. Would I have been right? Or would I have been right?"

Stonehenge nodded.

"Yes. John Dee referred to Kelley as his *scryer.* Therefore *ScryTech.* Kelley communicated with the spirits—he 'read' or 'scried' a crystal. It was an eye between the worlds. I assume that AFFA find this sort of obscure wordplay amusing."

"Amusing? My fucking sides are splitting."

I walked over to the window and looked out at the rain. I had a hopeless sort of feeling about this. It seemed ludicrous. Ridiculous. Hilarious. Stuff like that. Amusing? Oh, for sure. I reached inside my pocket and got my wrap of cocaine. I racked up a line and dealt with it quickly and efficiently. Stonehenge watched me, his eyebrows maybe raised a little. Well, I didn't care. He could raise them up to his hairline if he liked.

"Why me? You said something about finding out how 'reliable' I was. Something like that. But why the hell did you have to pick on me in the first place?"

I felt pretty strongly about this.

"Why not? Barry knew who you were. You're a private investigator."

"So if Barry hadn't caught me with Karen, I'd have been left alone? None of this would have happened?"

"All of this would have happened. If Barry hadn't been, um, introduced to you, so to speak, you might not have been directly involved with us, no. But we probably would have used you anyway. Your name's in the phonebook, after all. There aren't too many private investigators in the city. And once we found out you were going to be framed for something you didn't do . . . well."

This was bad. I guess I'd known that no good would come of sleeping with Karen. At least she hadn't made me fill up a specimen jar. Well, not as far as I knew, anyway. I did another line, and walked over to the couch. I sat down next to Stonehenge.

"So," I said in one of my most pissed-off voices, "what is all this about me being arrested for some kind of bizarre murder scenario on Monday? The Karen connection again, I guess?"

"I'm afraid so. A sacrifice is indeed planned for the early hours of the 13th of July. The anniversary of Doctor Dee's birth. But the date isn't really important. AFFA have been sacrificing human beings for centuries. Some of the victim's—er—internal organs are needed for one of Their alchemical actions. Obviously such a horrendous crime cannot be seen to go unpunished. Karen suggested you as the fall guy."

As he was saying this, Stonehenge poured himself another drink. Quite a small one, given the circumstances, I thought.

"Well, that's nice," I said, "that's really good of her. Considerate, even. Thanks, Karen. At least she remembered me, hey?"

Stonehenge sipped at his whiskey. He didn't say anything. Nor did I. I couldn't believe it. *Karen.* I felt sadder than I thought I could manage. I used my mouth to smoke a cigarette. I thought about innocent little flies caught in big sticky webs, and about the sad, muffled buzzing sound they made as the spider cocooned them in silk.

"And at least she didn't pick me to be the murder victim. I can think about that, and it makes me feel better. Not much better. They're really going to knock someone off?"

Stonehenge shrugged his shoulders.

"It's not like it'll be the first time. They've been killing people for years. For centuries, as I said. I've done some research into excavations that have gone on at the city Baths at various times. During one excavation, back in 1882, more than sixty skeletons were found. Only two of them were complete. The rest were . . . scattered. There were what looked like saw marks on the bones. As if they'd been . . . well, you can imagine. And there were some Saxon ovens found nearby. The ovens had human heads in them."

My mind felt like it was lurching from side to side. "What else?" I asked in a voice that didn't sound much like mine.

"I also tried to find out if any strange murders—I mean, this is real Jack the Ripper type stuff we're talking about—had taken place over the last couple of centuries, because you'd have thought that they would have been reported in the newspapers. Locally and nationally. And if you look hard enough—as I did—you can find them. But there's always something odd about the cases. The guilty party is always found, and is always . . . too obvious. It's like reading a badly written murder mystery."

"Any idea who they're going to kill?"

"Not a clue. Barry tried to find out from Karen, but he thinks even she doesn't know. I would imagine that kind of decision is taken at the very highest level."

"You're saying that there is an elite within the elite? A boss or whatever?"

"I would think so. Barry says there is, but again, it's one of the things that he doesn't get told."

"However many specimen jars he fills."

Stonehenge looked uncomfortable. He took another sip of whiskey. Suddenly I remembered Kafka's message on the answerphone. Call him. Urgently. My watch said 10:15 P.M. Okay. I picked up the phone and dialled his mobile number.

"Colin? Yeah, it's me. Yeah. I got your message. That's why I'm phoning, you dope. Yes, I have been busy. I've been very fucking busy. Can you get over to my office? Look, just come over here. I'll tell you when you get here, okay? I'm not talking about any of this over the phone. Well, if 'paranoid' means feeling that people are out to get me, then yes, I fucking well am. You'll be here in ten minutes? Okay." I slammed the phone down. I turned back to Stonehenge.

"My contact is coming over. You cool about that?"

"Who is your contact?"

"A guy called Kafka. Colin Kafka. He's a hack on the local rag, but he's kosher. I know him from way back. He knows something's going on and he knows that it's dodgy. He arranged my meeting with ScryTech. I told him about Charlcombe, too. We can trust him. Well, I'm pretty sure we can. It's not like we have a choice, anyway."

Stonehenge closed his eyes for a second or two.

"You're right. I'll stay for a while. But I have to go soon. Barry and I have work to do. There isn't much time . . . ."

He was damn right about that. My liberty was dripping away in front of me. I wondered what the hell I was going to do. This line of thought was becoming a habit. And it hadn't ever done me any good. Some more time passed. There was a knock at the door. I went over and let Kafka in.

He wasn't wet. "Has it stopped raining?" I asked him.

"Uh-huh. Stopped an hour ago. Maybe more."

I furrowed my brow. Anyway. The weather was the least of my worries.

"This is Colin Kafka," I said to Stonehenge. "Colin, this is . . . call him Stonehenge. He won't tell me his name. But he told me a whole lot of other stuff. Stonehenge, tell Colin what's going on. Colin? Sit down. I'll get you a drink."

Stonehenge talked to Kafka for a little while. I used the time to smoke some more cigarettes. I also paid attention to the way the hands moved on my watch. They moved forward. I couldn't do anything about that, but it wasn't good. I looked out of the window. It was raining.

Kafka made some surprised noises while Stonehenge filled him in. He didn't break anything though. Maybe that was just me. I put all my cocaine on the desk and split it into four piles. I scooped up each into a separate wrap. At one stage in his lecture, Colin held his hand out, holding his empty glass. I filled it for him. Stonehenge reached the end of his spiel.

"So it's true," said Kafka. "You're going to be arrested. Someone else is going to be murdered. Hey, Valpolicella. You get off lightly."

"It had occurred to me. Not as lightly as I'd like, though. What I'd prefer is that I get off. End of story." Then I told him about my day. My fun day, with all the great stuff in it. About the CCTV control room and more particularly about being followed, kidnapped, beaten up, and dumped in a field. He looked a little concerned about that, but I told him it was all in the past. I'd put it behind me. Then I told him that I'd got an idea.

"It's not very well thought out or anything, but it's all I've got. You don't get claustrophobia, do you?"

Kafka looked hard at me. "What do you want?"

"I want to go back down that hole at Charlcombe. And you're coming with me."

Kafka started to shake his head, but I wasn't standing for that kind of crap. I wasn't in the mood to argue.

"You want your fucking story? Come and get it. This isn't local. It's national. It's international. It's syndication. *Understand?*"

Kafka nodded, numbly.

"You're coming with me. You can borrow a flashlight and everything. See how generous I am? And you can have this, too." I passed him one of the little coke wraps. He walked over to the desk, emptied it out, and hoovered it up in one go. He inhaled again, deeply. He turned to me. His eyes were shining.

"I'll do it," he said.

CHAPTER 14

WHERE'S MY FLASHLIGHT?

There was something I thought I might need. And I remembered someone who might be able to help me out. I didn't have a number for her, but I could recall where she lived. It turned out that Stonehenge had a car, so I told him to get it. He was back inside ten minutes. I told him to take us up to the suburbs on the northern slopes of the city. An acquaintance of mine had a big house up there. She was a commodities trader or something. Whatever. She pulled in a lot of dough. But I had something on her. Ancient history, but it's good to keep a mental record of favours owed.

Stonehenge kept the engine running while I rang the bell. She was at home. She was surprised to see me. Not pleasantly surprised, but I persuaded her to let me in out of the rain. She was having some kind of dinner party or something, so we had to talk in the hallway. It was a nice hallway. Big. Elegant. I fitted right in. Oh, for sure.

We had a whispered conversation. She whispered furiously, which I didn't know was possible. Not as furiously as she managed it, anyway. I kept calm. I said that I didn't have a lot of time. I said I'd explain later. I said she didn't have to be involved, or connected. I said a few other things. I don't remember what.

Anyway, it must have worked, because I was ushered out four minutes later with a pistol in my pocket. She slammed the door as we drove off. I hoped her dinner party was a success.

Stonehenge took us further up the hill, then down a lane to Charlcombe. I checked out the gun. Okay. It was a gun, and it had some bullets in it.

"What the hell is that?" squeaked Kafka. I shrugged my shoulders. I didn't bother saying anything. I couldn't think of many words that wouldn't sound stupid. Stonehenge dropped us off at the bottom of a little track leading up to the church. We got out of the car.

"I'm not sure of the wisdom of this," said Stonehenge. "But there's no time to worry. Be extremely careful," he said, "and don't use your torches until you get down into the hole. I don't know what you'll find down there. What's your mobile phone number?"

I gave it to him.

"I'll telephone you at eight tomorrow morning. If you don't answer I'll call again at nine A.M. And again at ten A.M. If you don't answer any of these calls, I shall assume that I won't be seeing you again. Ever. If you find yourself in a tight spot, on no account mention Barry or myself. On no account. Understand?"

I nodded. He nodded back. He pulled the door closed after us, quietly. He wound down his window. "Good luck," he said. And he drove away.

I led Kafka along the lane for fifty yards or so, until we reached a gap in the hedge. The dig would be somewhere below us. I couldn't see it yet, but I knew it was there. We left the lane and picked our way through the wet grass. Colin was complaining about the rain. That was okay. The weather was the least of my worries. I saw the tarpaulins that covered the dig a little further down into the valley. It was a very still night.

No breeze at all. Only the continual whisper of the rain and, I thought, the beating of my heart. I think I was scared. It was getting cold. I guessed it was what, midnight? Or later. It was the witching hour. Thirteen o'clock, and I was going to climb down a sixty-foot deep hole that led to the underground domain of a cabal of power-crazed lunatics who figured they were about to control the world. It wasn't smart, what I was doing. It wasn't smart, and it wasn't clever.

We stopped at the edges of the tarpaulin. I told Kafka where the CCTV cameras were. I didn't tell him about my inkling that there were maybe infrared cameras down in the hole. I guessed that he knew enough already. I told him to be very, very quiet. We made our way, zigzag fashion, to the hole. Kafka was impressed. But not favourably.

"That's a . . . that is a very deep hole. We're going down—there?" he said quietly.

I murmured a yes. He turned to look at me, to give me some kind of hard stare or something, but it was too dark for anything like that to work. So I just made a gesture. My gesture said *let's go*.

I went first. I climbed down about ten rungs and waited for Kafka. He was a couple of minutes getting his courage together, or deciding whether or not to run away. I waited some more. Then I saw his legs coming down. I carried on. When I thought we were about fifteen feet down I clicked my flashlight on. The light was blinding at first. Then I could see. But I couldn't see much. The sides of the hole were wet. I could see pebbles lodged in the clay. I aimed the light downwards. The air in the hole was misty. I thought that I could just about see the bottom, but it was pretty much lost in the mist, which glowed yellowish in the glare. And I could smell that strange sulphurous odour again. Colin whispered down to me, "What's that horrible smell?"

"Don't know. It was the same last night though. It's sulphur or something. Come on. We're only about a quarter of the way down." I turned the light off.

The descent seemed to take an eternity. I got that feeling again, that there was nothing else in the universe than this hole, an endless tube through empty space. With two cold, wet humans in it. Both of them wishing they were somewhere—anywhere—else. I wasn't sure, but it seemed to me that the hole got narrower as we went down. It was about eight feet in diameter at the top, but if it got too narrow there wouldn't be enough room for both of us to stand at the bottom. It was going to be pretty damn cosy as it was. The smell was getting stronger, but then it seemed to fade. It was maybe coming up from the bottom of the hole in waves. The climb went on and on. My mind began to wander. Not surprising, I guess. I started to think about death. Death. You start to die the moment you're born. The whole of life is a series of close calls with death. Yeah, well. Whatever.

Finally I reached the bottom. There was more room than I expected. Kafka was just behind me. I stepped away from the ladder. I tried to speak as quietly as I possibly could.

"I'm going to turn the flashlight on. Close your eyes." I pushed the switch. The light was searing, but I forced my eyes to get used to it. Fuck. Where in hell were we? I had been right about the flagstones and the three tunnels. They stretched off into impenetrable darkness like three hungry mouths. But I'd been way wrong about there not being much space down here. We were in a kind of dome. Like we were in a bell jar with an impossibly long neck, which was the hole we'd climbed down. Or a gigantic chimney. I was sure it hadn't been like this the night before. I was certain. I remembered how I'd traced my hands around the walls, just by turning around pretty much on the spot. Now we were standing in a circular chamber maybe twenty feet in diameter. It was as if the beam from my flashlight had made the walls shrink away, or . . . it was crazy. Maybe we'd come down a different hole? Perhaps there were more than one, and I'd not noticed the night before? Or maybe KHS had dug out the base of the hole since last night?

Even as I was thinking up these increasingly desperate explanations I knew they were bullshit. Something weird was going on. Possibly it needed a better word than 'weird' to describe it, but I didn't have one to hand. And the smell was back, stronger than ever. It was horrible. Everything was so old it made my head hurt. I'd never been anywhere remotely like this before. It was old like—like a living thing could be old. Not like a place. I could almost feel its wheezing, impossibly aged breath sucking in and drooling out. There was mud and clay everywhere. The walls were made of it.

Dirty water dripped onto us from the sloping roof, and mud was scattered around in clumps and splattered on the walls. Pools of brownish, greyish water collected in puddles on the flagstones. And it was cold. The rope from the winch hung down with a big bucket, a bucket big enough for a body or two on the end of it. I looked at Kafka. His face looked terrible. The yellowish light didn't help, but he looked really bad. I wondered if I looked as bad as he did. Worse, probably. Yeah, well. I wasn't aiming to make a good impression anywhere. Not for the foreseeable future. I asked him if he was okay, and he shook his head slowly. He drew his finger across his throat. I knew how he felt. I wanted a cigarette badly, but I thought that I'd better not. I pulled my half-bottle from my pocket and took a deep swallow. I passed it to Kafka. He had what looked like an even bigger swallow.

I slowly swept the torch around the chamber, pausing the beam briefly at each tunnel entrance. There wasn't a sound. Just a terrible, terrible silence. I never felt less like whistling a tune in my life. I had no idea which tunnel we might walk along. My sense of direction was back at the office. The sulphur smell came and went. Water dripped down on us.

"Which tunnel?" I asked Kafka, not expecting him to have any firm thoughts on that one. He just stared at me. Okay. I pointed at random. "Let's take that one," I said flatly. I mean, for fuck's sake, they all looked the same. Kafka looked hopelessly at me, pulled a tape recorder from his inside pocket, and pressed record. He slipped it into his bag. We started walking.

The darkness of the tunnel closed in on us instantly. The beam from my flashlight struggled to penetrate the gloom. The dark in here was thicker, like it was treacle. I glanced back. The chamber was hardly visible, and we were only a few steps inside the tunnel. It was like walking into a coffin. The walls of the tunnel were the same as the chamber—semi-smooth mud or clay. There wasn't any trace of spade or pick marks on it. Maybe some sort of machine had hollowed it out.

"Let's try another tunnel," I muttered to Kafka. I don't know if he heard me. We bumped into each other, but I think he got the idea. We turned back into the chamber. Horrible as it was, it was less unpleasant than the tunnel.

"I'm having some second thoughts, and a hell of a lot of them," said Kafka in a strangled sort of voice. I gave him more whiskey. And then some more. I might have had some, too.

"Okay. That was horrible. I agree. Maybe the other tunnels won't be as bad," I said. I noticed that I didn't sound too convincing. "Let's have some Charlie and see how we feel after that." I opened the second little wrap and dipped my finger in the powder. Kafka did the same, and we rubbed it into our gums. I put the empty wrap in my pocket, had another swig of whiskey for luck, or something, and started towards another tunnel. Five steps into it I got the same feeling. We turned around and went back into the chamber.

"Right. Let's try the last one," I said.

"Which one is that?" asked Kafka.

I had no idea. We had been a few paces down two of the tunnels. One of them was right behind us. But which of the others we'd tried, I couldn't say. My loss of direction was total.

"Well, which do you think?" I whispered.

"I haven't got a fucking clue, and that in itself worries the hell out of me. That one? Or that one? What *is* this place?"

I couldn't answer him. I didn't know. It was that simple, and that complicated.

"That one," I said decisively, and walked towards the gaping darkness. This time we weren't turning back. This time we were going to find out what these tunnels were all about. This one was the same again—a ghastly, cloying, terrifying darkness of a sort I'd never known anywhere before. An intermittent dripping from the roof. I could feel the flagstones beneath my feet. My flashlight revealed nothing but the walls of the tunnel receding maybe ten feet or less before being devoured by the darkness. We walked slowly on. Nothing changed. Nothing at all. The silence got so fucking silent that it started to mess with my head. I stopped.

"Did you hear anything?" I asked, with a very clear idea of the answer I'd like to have heard.

"I don't—think—so," whispered back Kafka. Wrong answer. Not badly wrong, but wrong enough.

"What d'you mean, you don't *think* so?"

"Well, did *you* hear anything?" hissed Kafka.

"I don't know," I said. "Maybe. But I think it's this place. The quiet. Playing tricks on me. And you, too, by the sound of it." Yeah. Somewhere there was a rational, scientific explanation for this. But it wasn't down here. It wasn't where we needed it. We carried on, even more slowly. The smell came back again, nauseatingly strong. For a split second it reminded me of death, of putrefying corpses, animal and human, piled up and up and rotting, like some kind of infernal compost . . . .

I tried to force the thought out of my head but it wouldn't go. The fetid black liquid seeping from the crushed carcasses at the bottom of the pile, the writhing masses of larval flies, the sickening miasma emanating from it . . . . I stumbled against the wall and sank to the floor. I dropped the flashlight and clamped my wet hands to my face, I bowed my head and gritted my teeth, and I tried to force the horrendous vision from my mind. But it got worse. And I think I passed out, because the next thing that happened was Kafka slapping me in the face. I woke up and grabbed his hand before he hit me again.

"What the *fuck* . . . ?"

"Shit, you just, you just collapsed. You dropped the torch and it went out and fucking hell it was so dark . . . . I found mine and turned it on and you were just, well, you were out. I mean I, I almost fucking lost it, I almost panicked and lost it, so I started slapping you . . . ."

"Well, cheers for that. There was some stuff in my head that was far, far worse than being slapped. Thanks. Thanks a lot."

I was gasping. My gratitude was genuine.

"No problem. I don't mind saying I almost shat myself when your torch went out. Do the same if it happens to me. Bring me out of it, whatever it is. What happened?"

"You do not, *do not*, want to know. Let's just carry on. Where's my flashlight?"

"I dunno. I think it went over there somewhere." Kafka gestured with his light. The beam raked the floor around us.

"Maybe it rolled. There's a sort of slope to this tunnel."

"Yeah, maybe it rolled. So, let's see where it rolled to."

I felt almost better. I was pissed off at having lost it badly enough to pass out. If Kafka hadn't been there I could have lain there for hours. Being an independent operator was one thing. Lying out cold in a hellhole God knows how far beneath the earth is another. I shook myself. Maybe I said, "Let's go," or something. But we were walking on, further down, into the dark.

After a time, Kafka whispered, "Where's your fucking torch?" We hadn't found it. We'd walked a few hundred yards I guess. But no flashlight. It couldn't have rolled this far.

"Maybe we missed it. Maybe it got stuck in a niche or something. Rolled up against a rock. I don't know."

"What was that?" Kafka said.

"Sssh."

There was a sound. It was very quiet. But not as quiet as silence. Like a low, droning mechanical chant. An indistinct murmuring. It was coming from somewhere ahead of us, in the dark. Fighting every urge of self-preservation we walked towards it.

"Turn off the light," I said in a low voice. "Don't say anything at all."

Colin killed the flashlight. The darkness was suffocating. The sound was still there, moaning from somewhere. I trailed my hand against the wall to keep some idea of where I was. The surface was wet and slick, and sort of ridged under my fingers. It was very cold. Like something dead.

Nothing happened for a time. We were walking. The sound was droning, with slight variations in its tone. It didn't seem to be getting any louder. Then the wall disappeared. My hand touched nothing. I pulled my hand away as if it had been burnt. I grabbed for Kafka, and he stopped.

"Okay," I said in a voice only one notch above silence and one degree from panic. "Point the light at the floor. Turn it on."

A couple of agonising seconds passed while Colin felt for the switch. Then a blurry circle of flagstones was illuminated. But faintly. As if the batteries were dying.

"Right. Move the beam—slowly—so it points to the right of where I'm standing."

The illuminated circle travelled across the floor and up the wall, then forward along it. Where my hand had been was another tunnel, leading straight off to the right. The beam lit it only for three feet or so.

"Shit," I whispered. "Shine it at the other side." The light moved back across the floor and up. There was an identical tunnel the other side. I let out a long, slow breath.

"What are we going to do?" It was Kafka. His voice sounded controlled. Almost too controlled. "If this is some kind of maze . . . ."

"Then we're okay so long as we just keep straight on. If we don't take any turnings then we're . . . okay," I ended, limply.

"All right. We'll walk straight on. For another ten minutes. Then we turn round. We get out," he said firmly. "Ten minutes. Then we leave." There wasn't much room for argument in his tone. I didn't feel like arguing anyway. We walked. The droning chant carried on at the same almost inaudible volume. Kafka kept the flashlight switched on, aimed at the ground. There were a lot of flagstones down here. Whoever had built this had been serious about it. I kept my hand trailing on the wall. After a while there was another absence. We stopped. Moved the light around a bit. There were another two tunnels off, one at each side. And the beam from the flashlight was definitely fading.

"Right," murmured Kafka. "That's enough. Let's go back."

It was then that we heard another noise. Squealing. Distant, but a lot of it. It was like, I don't know, children. It sounded like children. A lot of children. But not human children. There was something unearthly about it. Like the squealing of hungry children, blind, hairless children who'd never seen the sun. Who knew they were getting fed soon. And it came from somewhere behind us.

I seized Kafka's arm and pulled him sideways, along the left-hand tunnel. And we ran. We just ran. The squealing seemed to be getting louder, and we just ran. The tunnel wasn't straight, not like the one we'd walked down. It curved around all over the place, and we careened off the muddy walls every few feet. The floor was sloping upwards now, slightly, but enough to notice that the running was getting to be harder work. We came to a fork in the tunnel and for no reason took the right-hand turn. And after a couple of hundred feet the floor stopped and there were steps going upwards. We didn't stop. I don't know how far behind us the squealing was, and I didn't care. We plunged up the steps, which wound in tighter and tighter circles until it was obvious we were running fast up a spiral stairway. I don't know where I got my energy from. Terror, I guess. The steps went on and on, until I smacked my head on something hard. I fell back against Kafka, but somehow he caught me and we stumbled on the stone steps beneath what felt like wood.

"It's a trapdoor," shrieked Kafka, "push against it! Push it!"

I got my upper back under the wood and pushed as hard as I could. Kafka squeezed up next to me and added his strength. Suddenly, with an ancient sucking sound, the trapdoor flipped up and slammed over. We scrambled out, grabbed the door and swung it back over the hole. It shuddered tightly over the darkness and we sat splayed over it, heaving with exhaustion. I think Kafka puked on the floor. I didn't feel too good myself.

I sensed that we were in some kind of room. Nothing else registered for a while. We sat there, gasping, wheezing, puking. And then everything was still. We slowly got our breathing back into some semblance of normality. A lot of puffing and blowing, but nothing too bad. Eventually I thought I'd use some of mine to speak.

"What, in the name of hell, was that?"

"I don't know," Kafka managed to say, "and I don't give a fuck. Where are we?"

It was a good question.

"Why didn't you use that fucking gun?"

Another good question. My answer, that I'd forgotten about it, was so stupid that I didn't let it out of my mouth. But anyway, it wouldn't have done any good. I didn't know what to shoot at. I didn't know where it, or they, were. Whether bullets would have worked. That place seemed beyond guns. The bullets would probably have slowed down, or fallen to the ground straight from the mouth of the barrel, or turned back at us. I didn't know.

"I don't know. Have you still got your flashlight?"

"Yeah. It must have got itself turned off."

"Well, turn it back on." He did. I almost wished he hadn't. We were in a room, okay. I'd been right about that. A room lined with incredibly dusty, cobwebbed coffins. Dust was everywhere. No one had been in here for a very, very long time. They hadn't thought to employ a cleaner. The inhabitants wouldn't have appreciated it anyhow. I noticed that the beam from the flashlight was bright. The batteries were fine.

"This is nice," I said. "Comparatively speaking. Quiet clientele. Peaceable."

"What the fuck is wrong with you?" spat Kafka harshly. "We're in a fucking crypt, fuck knows where, and you sit there making smart remarks. How are we going to get out of here, you moron?"

Much as I dislike being called a moron, especially by a reporter, I could see that he had a point. We were, as he had so helpfully pointed out, in a crypt. I had an idea that crypts were not good places to hang around in. We were going to have to do some more physical exertion. There was a door at the end of the room, which was a sort of coffin-lined corridor.

"You're right." The phrase was getting easier for me. "We've got to bust out of that door. But first, maybe we should put something heavy over this trapdoor."

"Like what?"

I just swept my eyes around the crypt.

"You're kidding me? Surely?"

I shook my head. "Remember that noise?"

Kafka nodded. He closed his eyes for about a minute. Then we manhandled a coffin off the shelves and placed it diagonally across the trapdoor. It wasn't a nice thing to do, but it didn't rate too badly in the context of the last few hours.

"Okay. Let's get the hell out of here," I said finally. I tried the door. It must have been bolted from the outside. Probably padlocked, too. I cast my eyes about, looking for something to try to lever it open with. No dice.

"It's going to have to be brute strength, Mister Kafka," I said. So we took turns at ramming the door. Repeatedly. We'd got a little panicked about being trapped in a crypt with a lot of dead folks, and having just used one of their number's final resting place as a kind of doorstop against unspeakable subterranean horrors, when I remembered about the two wraps of coke I still had left. So we dealt with those and finished the whiskey. It was all or nothing. We smashed against the door without a thought about how this might damage our shoulders. And eventually it started to give. We rammed into it harder until we shot out into fresh air and wet grass. And dawn light. And rain.

We lay on the grass staring up at the pale grey sky with the delicious rain falling on our faces for about a minute before we both simultaneously scrambled up and wedged the door shut again. We were outside a church.

"Let's get far away from here," said Kafka in one exhaled breath. I was with him on that. We walked smartly away from the door, across a graveyard, and jumped down a wall on to the pavement. I looked up at a noticeboard, and then further up at the pinnacles of the church tower.

Saint Stephen's Church," I said. "We're halfway up Lansdown Hill. Halfway back to the city from Charlcombe. That spiral staircase must have started hundreds of feet down."

"No shit, Sherlock," answered Colin. "And I'm never climbing it again. Full stop. End of fucking story. End of story. This is it, Valpolicella. No more. I thought I was sticking my neck out dealing with those lowlifes at the Lud Club. But they were a fucking breeze. They were great people."

We were walking down the hill. We could see the city, veiled in grey, below us. Just a couple of early rising fresh-air enthusiasts, that's what we were.

"From now on I'll help you, but strictly from a research perspective. However much cocaine you show me, I'm not doing any more fieldwork. No siree fucking Bob."

I just nodded, silently. Again, I wasn't in any kind of mood to argue. We walked down the hill, and I almost didn't mind the rain.

CHAPTER 15

PIGS

We parted at the junction near my flat. I wanted to go back there, and pretty badly. Kafka didn't say where he was going, but I guessed it would be somewhere with a bed. I let myself into my pad and crashed. I didn't have any desire to do anything else. But I couldn't sleep. That droning, moaning chant filled my mind. Round and round. I couldn't get it to shut up. Another thing was bothering me. Why hadn't there been any rats? Underground passages and rats went together like grand buildings and tourists. And that squealing. That hadn't been rats, for sure. What had it been the sound of? That horrible, unearthly sound that was like hungry children?

And then it came to me. Pigs. When I was a kid I'd had to walk past a pig farm on the way to school. And that was the same sound. Pigs. Did pigs eat rats? Not that I knew of. But pigs, a hundred feet underground? It didn't make sense. Well, yeah. For that matter, none of this whole business made sense. Not the kind of sense I was used to, anyway. I gave up the idea of sleep. It was properly light outside now. I got up and splashed my face with water.

My eyes didn't look so good, so I closed them and turned away from the mirror. I looked at my watch. For a couple of seconds I couldn't focus, but then it swam into view. Nearly 7:30 A.M. Sunday morning. Not much time left. I remembered that Stonehenge was going to call at 8. The battery on my mobile was nearly down, so I plugged it into the charger. I tried to eat a piece of toast, but it tasted worse than cardboard. I resigned myself to a few mugs of instant coffee.

I sat on the edge of my bed and reviewed the events of the last few hours. Moving walls? Probably. Eerie, horrifying sounds? Definitely. And pigs. Well, probably pigs, anyway. Miles of tunnels. I dug out my *A–Z* and tried to work out where we'd been. The dig was more or less directly south of the church at Charlcombe. The church crypt that we'd escaped at was . . . south again. I grabbed a magazine, and used it as a ruler to draw a line from the dig straight down. The Circus was dead south from the dig. Saint Stephen's Church, where we'd come out at on Lansdown Hill, was a notch or two off the line. That would account for the left-hand turning and the curving stairway. Interesting.

Stonehenge had said that there were three tunnels from a chamber below the Circus. And a few miles due north was another chamber, also with three tunnels radiating from it. Where all these tunnels led to didn't bear thinking about. I couldn't imagine how far they might go. And what was that horrible darkness, that seemed to consume light? It almost had texture. A really disgusting texture.

CHAPTER 16

EFFICIENT AND DECISIVE

I sat there for a little while, drinking coffee and smoking cigarettes. Then my mobile rang. I went over and unplugged it from the charger.

"Valpolicella," I said tonelessly.

"Hello. I'm glad you're still with us." It was Stonehenge's voice. It was exactly 8 A.M.

"I'm still alive, if that's what you mean. But it was a close thing. Probably."

"Is Colin still—with us?"

"He is. Sort of. He says that he doesn't want to be directly involved any more, though. It was pretty spooky. It was the pigs that really got to him."

"Did you say—*pigs*?"

"They sounded like pigs. We didn't know what they were at the time. I figured it out later. Hell of a noise. Sounded like hungry devil children to us. But I think it was pigs. Lots of them."

"That is extremely likely. Are you able to meet? Soon?"

"*Am I able* to meet? My life is full of meetings. Meet this girl here, that guy there, do this, go there. I can't remember when I last made a decision unaided."

"I'll be in Parade Gardens at nine A.M. Do you know where that is? I'll be sitting in a deckchair by the bandstand. All right?"

"Mm-hmm. I'll be there. Haven't got much else to do. Might as well turn up. Talk to you for a while."

"Will Mister Kafka be with you?"

"I'll give him a call, but don't count on it."

"Goodbye, Valpolicella." The connection was terminated. Okay. I put my mobile back on charge. What was that I'd said to myself? I was going to be the one pulling the strings? Yeah, right. Oh, for sure.

Parade Gardens is a park down in the city, next to the river, where old folk hang around on striped deckchairs waiting for the good old days to come around again. Why the hell Stonehenge wanted to meet there, I couldn't be bothered to work out. I lay back on my couch and watched the ceiling. I think I might have slept. Whatever, I was unconscious for a time. I woke up fighting a cushion and my jacket bunched up painfully under my arms. It was my mobile that woke me. I reared about like someone in a straitjacket until I finally located my phone somewhere behind my shoulder blade.

"What? Who?" I mumbled.

"It's Colin. I've got some disturbing news. Are you free?"

"No. Yes."

"What?"

"Never mind." I fumbled around some more and got my cigarettes. "Yes, I'm free, if you can call it that. What time is it?"

"Almost nine."

"In the morning?"

"Yes, in the morning. Can you meet?"

"What is this? Of course I can meet. I do very little else but meet people and get into trouble. In fact, I'm supposed to be meeting Stonehenge in about a minute down at Parade Gardens. He'll be wearing a deckchair so's I don't miss him."

"Right then. I'll see you there right away. Bye."

It seemed like everyone was being all efficient and decisive except me. Phoning up on the dot. Coming out with sentences like 'I'll see you there right away . . . .' Good grief. I rearranged my clothes, lit a cigarette, did some swearing, and walked as fast as I could be bothered to down to the Gardens. I saw Stonehenge from the balustrade overlooking the park. He wasn't in a deckchair because it was raining. Of course. Him and Kafka were the only people fool enough to go to a park in a downpour. They were standing in the bandstand, and by the look of it they were waiting for me. I wandered down with what I hoped was a nonchalant swagger. But it was probably obvious it was an exhausted wobble.

"Hello Colin and hello Stonehenge. This is nice. Fresh air. Weather."

"It was fine until about five minutes ago," said Kafka.

"Oh, sure it was," I said bitterly, "now why don't we go somewhere dry? That serves coffee? Chairs, tables, clean ashtrays, that sort of thing? There's a place just over the road. Come on."

I was pleased with myself. I was in charge. In control. It was a good feeling, even if it was only to do with where we drank coffee. They followed me through the rain to the café. It was empty, so getting a table wasn't a problem. I ordered coffee and toast. I figured it was worth giving food another try.

"Okay," I said as we waited. "Colin, you have some disturbing news. And don't tell me—Stonehenge has some disturbing news, too, am I right?" Stonehenge nodded. "I thought so. A double helping of disturbing news for Mister Valpolicella on this wet July Sunday morning. I am so pleased. I was just dreading anything nice. It would be hard trying to adjust, for one thing." I blew out a plume of smoke and stared at them. "So, who wants to go first?"

They looked at each other. Kafka spoke. "What happened last night was probably the most frightening thing I've ever encountered. I don't know what I was expecting, but . . . I tried to sleep when I got home but I couldn't. Too much in my brain. I couldn't forget the darkness, and I couldn't forget those—those horrible sounds. Then I realised that my tape recorder was still running. I rewound the tape. I felt like my memory was, I don't know, rewriting itself or something. I thought that maybe we hadn't heard anything at all. That we'd got sort of hysterical and imagined it."

I raised my eyebrows. Oh, so that was okay, then. We'd imagined it. I bowed my head and gave my temples a squeeze. I gestured for Kafka to carry on.

"Well, anyway. I had to get my head clear about whether we'd heard anything or not. So I rewound the tape and had a listen. It started off okay. I could hear us whispering and there was ambient noise from us wandering about inside that chamber. But pretty soon, when we were walking along the corridor, there was this weird noise. It started way before we noticed it. It was chanting of some kind, but it was really distant. By the time the tape picked us up, whispering about it, it had been going on for nearly twenty minutes. We just hadn't heard it at all. I couldn't make out what the words were. I think they were in another language. Something like, '*memvola sintrompo, memvola sintrompo, kontentiga morto, kontentiga morto.*' But the worst thing was, amongst all the gobbledegook chanting that I couldn't make sense of, there was your name. Repeatedly. *Martin Valpolicella. Martin Valpolicella.* Like they were calling you. As if they knew you were there."

"I never heard that. I never heard that. I did *not* hear that," I said, and I could feel sweat pricking on my scalp. I felt very cold.

"Nor did I, Martin. *But it was on the fucking tape!* I swear it. Look, I don't know myself what the hell it means. But the tape picked up stuff that we didn't hear. This Latin or whatever the fuck it was, it's there, on the tape. And your name. There is some extremely heavy-duty sinister shit going on, Martin, and whoever's doing it . . . I don't know. But this tape scared me, maybe as much as being in the tunnel scared me. It sounded— evil. I could hardly bear to listen to that noise on the tape. But I get the feeling that you're being trapped. The tunnels are a trap. You're walking into it. If I was you I'd take a hard look at what I was doing. I'd leave it all well alone . . . ."

"That wouldn't necessarily solve anything," said Stonehenge. I smoked my cigarette and looked out of the window. Their voices were just wallpaper. I looked out and I watched the raindrops running down the glass. I could see the woods on the other side of the valley, hazy in the rain. Everything looked calm. Hardly anyone walked past the café, and those who did were huddled up against the weather. In couples or alone, they passed by, on their way to the next episode in their lives. Sunday dinner somewhere, maybe. The cinema. The rain veiled the horizon, and I felt like I was inside a cloud. My eyes began to lose focus. I was drifting away. With a conscious effort I pulled myself back to wherever I was supposed to be. Stonehenge and Kafka were looking at me quizzically.

"What?" I asked a little bitterly. The brief escape had been pleasant. Maybe the best thing that had happened to me in a while.

"I was saying we mustn't frighten ourselves," said Stonehenge. "If we do, we're doing Their work for Them. They'll have won before we've begun. They'll have scared us off. And if this tape really does reveal that AFFA are calling your name, so what? They know it already. It doesn't mean they know you were there, though of course they may well have known, or been alerted somehow that you were there. AFFA already plan to use you as Their fall guy. The chanting might have been to do with that. There are less than twenty-four hours until the time that's been set for your arrest. I suggest to you both that we use this time as productively as possible, rather than getting tied up in knots over what may have sounded terrifying but probably, in reality, was not."

He took a slurp at his coffee, and waited for one of us to respond. I kind of spluttered. Kafka replied in a taut squeal.

"Sounded terrifying? You weren't there, mister. It was more than terrifying. And that was before I heard the tape. I think we're in trouble, really bad trouble, and I think the quicker we leave this stuff alone the quicker we'll be able to have some kind of normal life. Get it?"

"I get it. But I don't think you do. I think you're so freaked out that you can't think straight. Listen. Scaring people is nothing to Them. It's a sideline. If, as you think, They knew you were there, why didn't They come and get you? AFFA know the tunnels inside out. If They knew you were there then They could have got you. Easy. No problem. But They didn't. Why not? It's my opinion that They didn't know you were in the catacombs. So, Valpolicella's name might have come up. So? They've already decided to use him as the scapegoat for their next human sacrifice. It's just coincidence that you were down there when they were chanting his name."

"Well, that's fine," I said, "and very reassuring. Okay. Okay, Stonehenge, here's my verdict. You are full of shit. And you're going to stay full of shit until you agree to come with me, into the tunnels, tonight."

"Christ, Martin, you can't be serious," said Kafka, almost shouting. We were still the only customers in the café. The waiters were looking at us with interest. I shot them a glare.

"Shut up, Colin," I said quietly. "Let him answer me." Stonehenge looked me in the eye for a time. Maybe a minute. Maybe a little less.

"You're on," he said. "I've never been more serious. Tonight is our last chance to stop AFFA. I'm coming. Colin? Are you coming?"

Kafka choked. He looked like he was close to spraying the table with coffee.

"No. I am not. I'm staying up here, thanks. Look, I don't mind finding stuff out for you. I don't even mind sticking my neck out for you. But I am *not* going back down there. I'm scared. I don't mind admitting it. Okay?"

"Okay, Colin," I replied. "And if my name wasn't already known to them, if they hadn't already planned where in the basket my head was going to land, I'd be right with you. But I've got to do this. Otherwise they're going to fuck me up and I won't even know why. I might be crazy already, but trying to figure stuff out after the event isn't my style. Now, Stonehenge. Let me get this straight. You and me are going underground tonight. Okay. That'll be just peachy. But let's not get ahead of ourselves. Colin's told me his disturbing news, and it was lots of fun. If I remember rightly, you had some disturbing news, too. So, do we get to hear it?"

I waved to one of the waiters for more coffee. The toast had got cold, but it wasn't any great shakes when it was hot either. I'd had a couple of bites, but the bread had turned to cotton wool in my mouth. It had taken a little while to swallow. My mouth was pretty dry anyway, for some reason. Yeah, well. I looked at my watch. 11 A.M. More coffee arrived, so I drank some of it while Stonehenge gave us his news.

"You said something about pigs," he said.

"I did," I answered.

"What? What the hell are you talking about?" demanded Kafka.

"That horrible squealing? The noise that really got us moving? That was pigs, I'm pretty sure. I realised when I got home. That's what a load of pigs sound like at feeding time."

I hoped I sounded as bored as I felt.

"So, yeah, Mister Stonehenge. What about them? What about the pigs?"

"Well, when you mentioned pigs on the phone, I knew it must be true. It makes sense. *This city was founded because of pigs.*"

"Just fuck off, why don't you," said Kafka.

"Ah, give the guy a break," I said. "It's maybe hard work being a professor or whatever."

"Thank you," said Stonehenge wryly. "Now. Listen. Just as there are arguments in science, in politics, there are arguments about history. You've heard the cliché about history being written by the winners, yes?"

I nodded for Stonehenge to continue.

"Well, the history you were, presumably, taught at school is simply *one* account of *many* that exist. Most of the history you were taught is the invention of the Victorians, of the builders of the British Empire; of course, it pleased them to interpret history as a succession of empires, of continuous development, of increasing scientific enlightenment. But *their* history is not the only history. The real history of *this* city—a history that predates the Romans, never mind the Victorians—is that Bladud, the son of a certain King Lud—the ruler of Babylon-on-Thames, or, as we now know it, London—was exiled from the royal palace because he contracted leprosy. Bladud, who had been destined to become king of England, became a humble *pig herder* after his exile, and if that were not humiliating enough, his pigs caught his leprosy from him.

"That city, the ancient city of Babylon-on-Thames, is rumoured to still exist, metres below the modern edifice, below the sewers, below the underground railways. And in that subterranean city, below Ludgate Circus and Farringdon Road, where the River Fleet still flows below the surface, live the Fleet Pigs. An ancient race of pigs who have existed underground for centuries, feeding on the various sorts of debris that fall through the layers down to old Babylon. They're said to steal and consume human children . . . adults disappear as well. Vagrants. Drunks. Addicts. The lost, the miserable. Nothing more is heard of them. It may be that these disappearances are the work of the Fleet Pigs . . . .

"The legends say that these pigs are the descendants of those Bladud was given when he was exiled, a thousand years ago, or more. The leper Bladud wandered westwards through the countryside with his leprous pigs, reviled and rejected by all who saw him. Until he came to *this* valley, the valley where *this city* now stands. In those days it was a valley of darkness, bounded by towering hills and high cliffs, where amongst the matted vegetation the exiled Bladud found black bubbling quicksands, steaming with unnatural heat . . . bright red rocks stained with the iron content of the spring waters . . . blood red . . . . He led his pigs into the waters. When they emerged they were *cured*—they were free of the curse of leprosy that had afflicted them. Bladud followed them into the waters, and *he* was cured, too. He founded the city on this site.

"But Bladud was a tyrant. His thirst for power was unquenchable. He ruthlessly destroyed those who stood in his way. He set up prison camps for his enemies on the hills around his new city. They were more like death camps. Most of the hills around here have never been excavated, but there was one small dig early in the twentieth century on Solsbury Hill, to the east of the city. In an area of just a thousand square feet, the remains of six hundred mutilated bodies were found. Smashed skeletons. The excavators were appalled. They'd never seen anything like it. Body upon body. Bone upon bone. Nowhere else in Europe—not until the twentieth century—has revealed massacres on such an immense scale. The finds suggest that the whole area was incredibly heavily fortified, and anyone—anyone—who disagreed with the regime was brutally disposed of. And I'm not talking about myths here. Barry Eliot has heard this from Karen. What I'm telling you forms part of AFFA's oral and written history. In other words—for all intents and purposes—it's true."

"What about the pigs?" asked Kafka.

"I'm getting to them. Bladud loved pigs much more than he loved people. He had been despised and exiled by humans. Pigs had become his only companions—his leprous pigs. The descendants of his first pig herd became his—his killing machines. *He bred pigs to kill.* They became like pig Rottweilers. Again, this is what Barry has heard from Them. Bladud would have his enemies crippled, their joints smashed, then thrown as living food to his pigs. These pigs thrived on live human flesh. Bladud's victims were thrown down deep holes—oubliettes, or 'forgetting holes,' they're called—onto ever-growing mounds of the dead and the wounded, as food for the pigs that roamed the catacombs beneath the city."

"*Mounds of bodies?*" I said, almost to myself. Putrefying corpses, animal and human, piled up. *The fetid black liquid seeping from the crushed carcasses at the bottom of the pile, the writhing masses of larval flies, the sickening miasma emanating from it* . . . . I lit a cigarette. I felt bad.

"That is a revolting story," said Kafka. "Are you suggesting that what we heard in the tunnels last night were the descendants of these—these fucking man-eating pigs? Because if you are, then you're even more of a lunatic than I thought you were. You can't seriously be thinking of going down there?" He turned to me. "Valpolicella, don't listen to this guy. He's fucking crazy!" Then he stood up. His chair crashed to the ground behind him. The waiters were really taking notice now.

"Who the fuck are you?" he bellowed at Stonehenge. Stonehenge did a pretty good job. He faced Kafka down. He just looked him in the eye until he backed away. Kafka picked up his chair and sat down again.

"I am not your enemy. As I told Valpolicella, I'm an academic. I teach pre-Roman history at the University of London. When I was first told this convoluted and, I admit, barely believable story by Barry Eliot, I reacted much as you did. Though I didn't knock my chair over. But the more I heard and the more I thought about it, the more convinced I became that it was—and is—true. I've always studied conventionally. I've never had much time for earth mysteries, ley lines, or crop circles. But there are just too many gaps in our understanding of the world. It's been said that modern science has one superstition—which is the notion of coincidence. The same holds true for all modern branches of learning. Anyway, you heard the pigs. I've heard *about* them, but I've never *heard* them. You're ahead of me there."

"Ahead of you?" said Kafka incredulously. "And if we hadn't got any fucking further ahead then we'd have been eaten by the fucking things. Well. If you're right, which I seriously doubt, then you're still a lunatic. An ancient cabal of power-crazed killers, protected by flesh-eating pigs, a hundred feet below the city? And you're going to take them on?"

"We have to. Barry and myself are quite certain that this next sacrificial murder is to be part of one final ritual action that They must perform in order to get what they want—which is global dominion."

I put out my cigarette and counted the butts. Six. Probably time for me to say something. There was a handy gap in the conversation and it had my name on it. Only thing was, I wasn't sure what to put in it.

"Global dominion? Sounds pretty impressive. I guess a lot of people have fancied that over the years. Tried fairly hard to get it, too, I'd think. But none of them have got their hands on anything like it. Napoleon. The British Empire. Hitler. Stalin. No dice. They didn't make the grade. They had huge armies, a big heap of weapons, military prowess, intelligence, egomania. And still, they couldn't control the world. What makes you think that these AFFA bastards are any different?" Hey, that was good, considering I hadn't rehearsed.

"Two reasons. Time travel. And mind control."

I gaped at him. I nearly dropped my new cigarette. I almost inhaled a mouthful of coffee. I spluttered a little.

"You're straight out of the box, my friend. Not quite all connected up right. I mean, are you paying any attention to what you're saying, or are the words just coming out of your face?"

Stonehenge gave me a serious look. An exasperated look. Perhaps he really *was* a lecturer.

"They've been working on time travel for *centuries*. They perfected it in about 1950. Mind control was figured out a little later, in 1965 or thereabouts. The Philosopher's Stone, when used properly, when used absolutely accurately, enables *anything*. Anything at all. And obviously travelling through time has been a human fantasy forever. And after literally centuries of trying, They managed it. By using the Philosopher's Stone. And since the nineteen-fifties They've actually been *using* time travel. It's conventional to see the increasing pace of technological development as a natural by-product of human intelligence. But where do these random and rapidly increasing instances of technological inspiration come from? Why are they happening more and more, faster and faster? Coincidence? Synchronicity? Or something else? Who does not fear where this is all leading to? We see the signs—we see pollution, ever more dangerous 'accidents,' radioactivity, destruction of our world, extinction of animals . . . and those things are happening more and more, faster and faster, too. What has been happening during the last fifty years is the result of AFFA taking ideas from our modern world and giving them surreptitiously to carefully selected, highly placed people in the past. A damaged world is precisely what They desire. A world of frightened, desperate populations, a world of terrified slaves. Can't you see what kinds of trouble They have already caused?"

"I can see that I'm sitting in a café on a Sunday morning with an empty coffee cup in front of me. I can also see that it's nearly midday. And I can see that I'll find it easier to take this in if I've had a drink. Or three. So why don't we continue this fascinating discussion about . . . time travel . . . and . . . mind control . . . somewhere without three under-worked waiters listening to every fucking word we say? I'm beginning to feel like I'm on stage and the script is—well, it's really bad."

Kafka mumbled something unintelligible but I figured it was agreement of some sort. Stonehenge nodded, got up, and paid the bill to a smirking waiter. And we walked out into the eternal rain.

CHAPTER 17

BASICALLY VERY OUT TO LUNCH

The city on a Sunday was pretty much like it was on a Saturday. Or any other day. Loads of people. And about two-thirds of them were tourists filming and photographing just about everything they could. I guess they thought the rain was sort of quaint or something. Atmospheric. Romantic. They probably thought it was delightful. Yeah, well. I thought it might be delightful to get out of it.

We went past the City Hall, which made me a little nervous because of ScryTech being underneath it. I made efforts to avoid the ever swivelling CCTV cameras. The memory of being given a talking-to in that field up by the motorway was still vivid, despite the events of last night. My life was beginning to seem just a bit busy.

We hiked it a little way down an alley to a small pub. A very small pub. Stone fireplace, four tables, barstools. Some kind of inoffensive jazz playing low. It suited my mood better than a huge, echoing café. Colin arranged some chairs while I went up to the bar. Stonehenge got out his cigarette-rolling equipment. By the time I got back, they had both settled down. They were making strenuous efforts to avoid each other's eyes. Stonehenge was studying a wall. Colin was examining the ceiling. I realised that if anyone was going to get the joint jumping, it was going to have to be me. I kept my voice low, like the jazz.

"Hey there, Stonehenge. Good to be having a beer? Up here, in the city? Looking forward to meeting the pigs? Sure you are. Anyway, I've been thinking. And you'll be pleased to know that the direction these thoughts of mine have been taking is towards the notion of believing you. Just for now though, you understand. If I spend too much time at parties talking about man-eating pigs, time travel, and—what was the other one? Mind control, that's it—I'm going to lose friends faster than I do already. But, like I say, for now I've decided to believe you. The whole deal. You can say anything you like, and I'm right there, nodding like a little doggie. I've forgotten what I might have wanted to ask you. It doesn't matter though, because I seem to be in some kind of fantastical nightmare."

I took a holiday from talking to drink some of my beer and locate my cigarettes. I was bored. Listening to my own voice does that to me. The pub was filling up. I couldn't figure out why there were so many people around, given that this was the worst weather I could remember. Maybe they were all involved in their own bizarre missions.

"So you don't want to know any more?" asked Stonehenge.

I shook my head. "None of it seems to make anything any clearer. Right now I'm interested in staying out of police custody come tomorrow. If doing that means preventing someone being murdered—well, like I say, I'm a civilised guy. I'm all for stopping people getting dead. But if it means taking on a whole gang of crazies who are, like Colin pointed out, protected by equally crazy pigs, I'm not so sure that getting arrested isn't the easier option."

"You're wrong," murmured Stonehenge, "you're so wrong. Every sacrifice they carry out means they become more powerful. You know about sacrifices? You know why a human sacrifice is more useful to Them than an animal sacrifice? Any death means that energy is being released. Energy cannot be destroyed. It can only be transferred. At its most basic level, sacrifice is just energy transferral. A sudden or a violent death releases a lot of energy very quickly. If the people doing the killing are prepared to harvest that energy, if they have the means to do so, then that energy can be stored, used . . . it can be controlled as any form of energy can be controlled. It can be channelled. As any form of energy can be channelled. The more death, the more energy. Look at what happened to the global economy after the Second World War. And 9/11? Very, very good for business."

"Wait a minute," said Colin. He peered at Stonehenge through slitted eyes. "Are you asking us to accept that these people, these 'AFFA'—get their power through some sort of . . . transformer? That they can use death to . . . . Oh, for fuck's sake, I don't even know why I'm wasting my time here. Hey, Martin. Shall we leave this guy, who won't even tell us his name, to spout on to some other poor bastard? Because, because . . . I can't stand much more of this shit."

I gave Stonehenge a glance with upraised eyebrows. A quizzical look, you could call it. I'm quite good at them. Then I turned to Kafka.

"Colin, you're a reporter. No, I'm sorry. A *journalist*. An *investigative* journalist. You've been doing some investigating. And I can't see why you want to stop investigating so quickly. Why don't you finish the fucking job? Shit, I can even get you a gun, if you have any concerns that a gun might get rid of. How about you, Stonehenge? Think you might need a gun? I still know some useful people. I can get guns. Bullets. You know how to handle a gun, Stonehenge?"

He looked at me for maybe a minute, and then slowly shook his head.

"I can demonstrate. It isn't hard. We'll go out to the woods and I'll show you the business. Point and click. Technology at its purest. *Bam bam*. Bye-bye, bad guy. Or good guy, depending on where you aim the piece. Isn't that right, Colin?"

Kafka grunted unhappily. He looked at his watch. "Okay, okay . . . Valpolicella, you get the guns and the wherewithal to make them more than decorative. Stonehenge? Tell me some more . . . stuff. Background. All right?" Kafka got his notebook out, a display of professionalism I appreciated. Mentally I went through my contacts. Could I get hold of some guns? Probably. Maybe. I worried about this for a time. Stonehenge was talking to Kafka. I started to listen. Despite my better instincts.

"AFFA are seeking a new world. A new world order, to coin a cliché. They want to be like gods. *Gods*. The world we live in is too chaotic for Them. They don't like it. Leaders They appoint get deposed, or voted out. Laws They get passed are reformed. That's why they've been using the Philosopher's Stone to subtly alter perceptions over the course of time. That's why time travelling has always been so important to Them. If enough people have their perception altered, then that changed perception becomes reality. A new reality. So the Industrial Revolution, atomic energy, biological warfare, cloning . . . these are just ideas, right? Until they become reality. And then they are more, much more, than ideas. The idea that AFFA have has to do with total control. Total control means control of energy. For Them, energy is inextricably bound up with death. Take oil. Oil is nothing more than the black ooze left behind by the deaths of millions of organisms, millions of years ago.

"The new reality being prepared by Them is one of war, famine, and *death*. The end of consensus. A world controlled utterly, ruthlessly, by the spiritual descendants of King Bladud. What he achieved in this area of England will be worldwide. The apparatus has already been put into place. What we know as the military-industrial complex already exists. That's an integral part of what AFFA are creating.

"Metaphorically, which is probably the best way to make sense of Their objective, we are talking about the end of the republic. The beginning of the empire. The empire of AFFA. And you don't need me to remind you how it is that empires operate. Through ruthless suppression of opposition. Understand?

"We don't know what else is down beneath the surface. The oldest tunnels, the ancient tunnels, are straight down, directly beneath us, directly below the city itself. Maybe the rest of the catacomb complex is equally old. Like Charlcombe."

Colin had stopped writing. He was chewing on the end of his biro. "This is too much," he said, "too wild. I can't get this kind of stuff published. Apart from being basically very out to lunch . . . it's . . . . But if it's true . . . ."

He was sounding at least partly convinced. He was sounding like someone who was beginning to believe something he didn't want to believe.

"You can't prove anything . . . ."

"There's nothing to prove." Stonehenge was firm. "Why are you bothering with the idea of proof? It's too late, Kafka. The time for proof is over. It's time for action."

I had to say something. I was getting upstaged here.

"Republic, empire, whatever. Is any of this strictly relevant? Er, excuse me, no, it isn't. Is it random new age conspiracy bullshit, or is it some stupid concoction you've brewed up from terrible novels, wacko Internet sites, and I don't know what else? For all I know you might be telling the truth. For all I know you really are some academic from the big town. But listen. Everything that is connected with this seems to land on my doorstep. Not yours. Not Colin's. Not Barry's. Mine. Get it? It's *my* fucking problem, okay? And I think that we're approaching some kind of crisis point here. This is where it gets decided whether or not I get arrested for murder. *Do* the cops knock on my door tomorrow afternoon or not? Is there some unbelievably gruesome murder? *Or not?* Does this psychotic cabal of murdering bastards take over the world, or do I just get up in the fucking morning and put the fucking kettle on?"

I stopped talking for long enough to finish my pint. I lit a cigarette, too, but you're probably used to that. I hadn't killed the last one properly. It was still smouldering away in the ashtray. I kind of kicked it around with my little finger.

"And, to be frank, you're the last person I want to be relying on to provide me with any sort of answers. I've had enough. Enough fucking talk. Enough of it. So let's quit talking, hey? No more. Both of you, you come down into the tunnels tonight. Barry Eliot, too, okay? No more mysterious guy on the sidelines for Barry. That fucker is either in or I walk away. Clear?"

"No." Stonehenge spoke quietly. "Barry is going to be involved in tonight's action, yes, but not with us."

"You're kidding," I replied, "surely. What the hell's he going to be doing? Filling another specimen jar on stage, or what?"

"It's intended that he should wield the sacrificial weapon."

"Barry's going to kill someone? Give me a break. He's a golfer."

"He has to prove himself to Them. If he doesn't do it, They'll kill him instead. It's traditional."

"*Traditional?* That's *traditional*? Christmas is traditional. Or—I dunno, morris dancing. But compulsory participation in human sacrifice? What the fuck are you talking about?"

"The newest initiate has to carry out the killing. It's how They keep Their people under control. It's how initiates are bound to

Them. Through guilt, through fear, acquiescence, and then . . . agreement. Eventually, enthusiasm. Or else."

"Well, what in hell is Barry going to do? Is he going to do it? Kill someone with a knife, for Christ's sake? Look, how deep is he in?"

"He's in deep. Otherwise we wouldn't have the information we do. He wants to get out alive. I told you, he sensed that They were close to Their goal. He needed to stay involved to get the information we need to stop Them. But matters have escalated much faster than we could foresee. Which is why we decided to bring you into the equation."

"Yeah, well. You know how glad I am about that. I assume Barry would rather not cold-bloodedly kill some innocent victim, would rather not get any more involved with these people than he already is?"

"That's correct."

"And he's got this far, in order to get some information that will help unspecified outsiders—i.e., *us*—to put the kibosh on the whole deal?"

"Yes."

"Well, what in the name of fuck is this information? Because, Mister goddamn Stonehenge, we really fucking need it. No more messing about, okay? No more lecturing. We're going back down tonight. We three. We get Barry. We stop whatever it is that your subterranean mafia are doing. That's the plan, right? It ends with us being alive, yes? So, stop fucking about! What do you have?"

"I have a map."

"A map?" I was incensed. "We're setting ourselves up against insane, time-travelling killers protected by flesh-eating pigs, and we're armed with a fucking *map*? Are you completely mad?"

Stonehenge was quiet. Calm. Stuff like that. He spoke gently, as if to a dumb kid.

"Have you ever tried to go anywhere you don't understand without a map?"

Okay. I was speechless for a time. Then I was speechless for another time after that. I stubbed my cigarette out harder than was necessary. I got up. I went to the bar. I bought another pint, and I didn't smile at the barman. I went back to our corner table. Colin and Stonehenge were still there, much to my annoyance. I mean, for fuck's sake. What did we have? An academic, a reporter, and a private investigator. And a sperm-donating golfer. Sooner or later I was going to wake up. In the meantime it was all I could do to stop myself chucking my pint at Stonehenge and leaving the fucking building. It gets like that sometimes with me. Especially when I've had enough of a stupid fairground ride that I didn't want to get on anyway and ends up costing a lot more than I'd thought. I sat down. Eventually I calmed down enough to put my elbows on the table, raise my hands, and sink my face into them.

"That isn't all I have," said Stonehenge quietly. "We've also found out that there are vats of chloroethylene down there. Dry-cleaning fluid. Enormous containers of it. It's an extremely important part of Their alchemical processes."

My face stayed in my hands. I mumbled through my fingers.

"Dry-cleaning fluid? Enormous vats of *dry-cleaning fluid*? Well, shit, okay. After the pigs I can take anything. Just tell me quickly though, um . . . *why?*"

I noticed that Kafka was just staring at the table. He wasn't writing anything down. He had the look of someone who was barely tolerating the situation.

"Cosmic rays are continually bombarding our planet. Cosmic rays are the reason for the vats. Chloroethylene slows the rays down enough for them to be measured, analysed, and ultimately understood. Then the resulting data can be used . . . . There's no time to explain, and I doubt you'd have the patience anyway. But if we can destroy the vats, we'll have stopped Them, at least temporarily. If we can get Barry out, we'll mess up Their plans badly. If we can get Their victim out, then we've really slowed Them down. And, Valpolicella, that will mean that you don't get arrested. No murder. No blame. No culprit."

I looked up. This was the best news I'd heard for a day or so. No culprit? No big men in black uniforms kicking the door in? I was interested all over again.

"Mmm-hmm. Cosmic rays. From, er, the cosmos, presumably. Vats of dry-cleaning fluid. If you don't mind, I'll just ignore that for now. So, you have a map, presumably of the tunnels?" I asked. Stonehenge nodded. Colin looked up. I pushed on. "You know where these vats of cleaning fluid are?" Stonehenge nodded again. "You know where this, this . . . sacrifice is meant to take place?"

"I do."

"Do you seriously think we can pull it off? You really think we can stop these maniacs?"

Stonehenge looked around the pub for almost longer than I could bear. Then he spoke. "Last night, I would probably have said no. But while you and Kafka were in the catacombs, I did some more work on the information Barry had managed to get. And because Karen was very excited about AFFA's progress, and because Barry was more than usually . . . er, *willing* . . . well, between us we managed to gather a significant amount of useful information—the locations of the vats, and of the sacrificial altar."

"And a map of those fucking tunnels."

"Yes. This is, as I said, Barry's last chance to escape Their clutches. He is utterly serious about getting out. He stole a map from Karen. It was a last ditch gambit. If he's found out . . . ."

"He's dead," interrupted Kafka. "Like we are."

I stared into space. Somewhere in my heart there was a jagged hole, torn open. Karen. Barry. Me. I guess I was maybe more upset than I thought.

"Excuse me, but this has been all too far-out. I have to go and buy something to smoke." Kafka pointed with his thumb towards the cigarette machine by the stairs, but I glared at him. I needed to go away. The smokes were an excuse, sort of.

"I need a little time to let this, ah, information—sink in," I said, "but I've got attached to you guys. Strangely. Against my better judgement. How's about we meet up in a couple of hours? There's a pub just up from Charlcombe. At the top of Lansdown Hill. I'll see you both there at four P.M. Okay?" I got up and walked to the door. I glanced back. I couldn't see Stonehenge's face, but I could see Kafka's. I was already out in the rain, but for some reason I thought Kafka had been smiling.

CHAPTER 18

AN INTEREST IN GUNS

It felt good to be leaving the pub. Kafka and Stonehenge could talk about cosmic rays and I wouldn't need to bang my forehead on the table. I had a couple of hours to collect two guns. To stock up on whiskey and cocaine. But I wasn't going to think. No way. If I started doing any of that I would be getting on the next train out of town.

I was raising my eyes to the heavens, or somewhere with a nearby postcode. On the way up from the wet pavement to the wet sky, my eyes stopped. They stopped because they noticed a black camera twenty feet up a lamppost. Its lens was staring straight at me. I didn't stop walking. I remembered the speed of the visual mapping process. I considered myself to be of particular interest to ScryTech. Parts of me still ached from the advice I'd been given by those nice, smartly dressed men with the shiny shoes and the expensive car.

I ducked into a shop and very quickly picked up an umbrella before ducking out of it again. I figured being done for shoplifting wasn't something I should be worrying about. I was out of there and into a few other shops. I went through some places that had entrances front and back. I did my best to appear inconspicuous. The umbrella helped, once I was out in the rain again.

I did a pretty fast circuit of town, tagged along with some tour groups, and ended up getting on one of those open-topped double-decker buses that have recorded commentary in four languages about a whole load of tourist bullshit. I could have told the huddled tourists, steaming up the windows with their wet coats, a few things that weren't on the official itinerary. But I didn't. Yeah, well.

I got off at the Circus, one of the places that I'd noticed on the ScryTech map that *didn't* have CCTV. I walked over to the trees that grew above the grass in the centre. I thought about what Stonehenge had said about the place. Part of some giant sky-visible symbol. Whatever. There was a big metal manhole cover, or something like it, between the trees, right in the very centre of the Circus. The thought of what might be beneath the thin sheet of metal I was standing on gave me the creeps. Raindrops from the trees drummed on my new umbrella. I pulled out my mobile and dialled Kafka.

"Colin? It's Valpolicella. Are you still in the pub? Okay. When you leave, avoid the CCTV cameras. There's one right at the end of the lane. I didn't see it until it was too late. It got me, for sure. Don't let it get you. What? Yeah, yeah, but you can't be too careful. Look, if ScryTech do the CCTV for KHS then they could have your mug already. Yeah. Underground, maybe. No, I don't know for sure. I'm being cautious, okay? Yeah, I'm getting the, erm, implements next. I'm at the Circus. No, I don't think I was followed. What do you mean, at least it's stopped raining? Not here it hasn't. Yeah, yeah. See you at four P.M."

I trudged up the hill, locating a couple of bottles of whiskey at a shop near my flat. I thought of nipping in, getting some dry clothes, but I decided not to. It was probably watched. Or bugged. Surveillance cameras are very, very small these days. Anyway, I didn't have much time. If I went to the flat I might fall asleep, and I couldn't afford that luxury. No way. I couldn't remember the last time I'd slept. A bad sign. I really needed that cocaine. And some speed, if I could get it. Staying awake was going to be a priority from now on. Yeah, speed was a far better bet. Lasted a whole lot longer. Pharmaceutical amphetamine, that would do it. I had a hunch that one of my contacts would be able to sort me out.

My first call was to one of my acquaintances I knew through the investigation business. She'd employed me to find out what her rat of a husband was up to. Well, he was up to a lot. Apart from affairs (two, consecutive, both women involved very happy to tell me exactly what kind of rat he was) and prostitutes (too many to keep track of, almost continual, all willing to talk to me for cash donations), he'd also killed a young guy in a hit-and-run and was paying a reasonable wedge to someone who'd happened to notice his registration. The blackmailer was a rat, too. But that didn't concern me. Not on the job description. Everything turned out peachy for my client, which was why she lived in a nice grand house. She'd been very grateful for my services. For a while anyway. She also offered a high-class line in drugs to select friends and—well, acquaintances. Like me.

She wasn't too happy about giving credit to a wet and tired private investigator, but I guess she figured it was better than me getting all upset on her doorstep. She had a pistol I could borrow, too. I had a hot cup of tea in a basically very chilly atmosphere before I got the hell out of there. I needed another gun and a lot of bullets. It was irritating.

Okay. It was after 3 P.M. I needed to be quick. I had another contact in the area, a computer expert who was kind of a gun nut. He was the knucklehead who'd installed my system for the office a couple of years back. He was fascinated that I was an investigator. Amazed that I didn't carry a weapon as a usual thing.

He talked about guns a lot while he fiddled around with leads and hard drives and stuff like that. Very incautious talk, I remembered thinking at the time. Careless talk. I didn't like him much. In fact, I didn't like him at all. But I still had his card. It was in my wallet. So I knew where he lived. So that's where I went. It was a dismal looking place, a sort of 1960s detached house surrounded by dank conifers. His car was in the drive. I guessed he was in. I punched the doorbell a couple of times.

He came to the door wearing a dressing gown and a whole chinful of stubble. A moustache, too. I've always liked moustaches. In the same kind of way I like the familiar pools of vomit in the alleyway outside my office. He didn't seem to recognise me, so I flashed my card.

"Valpolicella. Private investigations. You installed my computer. Remember?"

He looked confused. "Um . . . yes . . . " he said slowly. "It's Sunday, Mister Valpolicella. Is this an urgent matter? Something wrong with the system?"

"Aren't you going to ask me in? Out of the rain?"

He did, with reluctance. I stepped into the hall. Something about it reminded me of my flat, except it smelled worse. But that sort of thing's a matter of taste, I guess. I dreaded to think what his bedroom was like, if the hallway was anything to go by.

"Can I offer you anything? Tea? Coffee?"

"You can offer me something all right, but it's not that."

"Is, er, something wrong with the, ah, computer?"

"Always. Everything. But that's not why I'm here. I seem to remember you talking about weapons. Guns, particularly. I take it you have an interest in guns? A big interest, I'd guess."

He looked uncomfortable, to put it charitably. His moustache bristled. I winced, not too obviously I hope.

"I have, as you say, an, um, ah, an *interest* . . . " he said, very carefully, "but all above board, all . . . ."

He had been going to say 'legal.' But I guessed it wasn't.

"Take it easy," I said flatly, "this isn't a bust or anything like that. Nothing to do with the law. Not yet, anyway. Not unless you want it to be. Guns aren't very popular with most people. I don't think the police take kindly to private arsenals." I was completely unthreatening. Well, okay, not completely. "I want you to give me a pistol. Right now. I'm in a hurry."

"I can't just give you a pistol!"

"Oh, yes you can. Bullets, too. And you're going to give them to me now." I guess there's just something about a man who's just been chased through underground catacombs by flesh-eating pigs and is looking at doing it all over again. Like I say, I wasn't being threatening. But my gun-loving computer guy put his face in his hands for a little while before reluctantly beckoning me through a door.

We passed through his kitchen. I didn't comment. Not many people could have suppressed an observation of some kind. But I kept quiet. I wanted a gun, not a discussion about domestic hygiene. He led me through another door into what would have been his garage. If it hadn't been full of weapons.

"This is interesting," I said politely, "very interesting. It's quite a serious interest you have here. Before you start justifying yourself or whatever, I'd like to remind you that I'm in a hurry. A big hurry. So, listen. You give me a gun, some bullets, and— wow—I forget I know you. Because I'm in trouble. You do not want to be involved. Hey, I wish you were, preferably instead of me, but you're not. So, get a move on."

This guy was very creepy. I'm no great shakes myself, and I'd had dealings with people who were no shakes at all. But this guy was off the scale.

"What sort of gun do you want?" he said, in a quiet voice.

"Something that fits in my hand and isn't too complicated to operate. I'm not a rocket scientist. Something that works first time, every time."

Yeah, well. He went off into a kind of monologue. He talked for about fifteen minutes. I tried to listen for a minute or two before I realised it was futile. He probably talked like this every night. Only this time he had an audience. Eventually he handed me a gun. Then some ammunition. He was still talking, while I was watching his hands. Shaking. He was scared of me. That was kind of weird, when I thought about it. He had more weaponry in one garage than I'd seen in my life, give or take a few of the more extreme scenarios. And he was scared of me. Still, he was just another lunatic. Anyway, I had places to go. Flesh-eating pigs to see. I had a busy life.

After tearing myself away, I wandered further up the hill in the rain towards the 4 P.M. rendezvous. I was going to be late. Recently my sense of time was having problems. Hours were getting shorter, and minutes just weren't in on the game. So, I got to the pub a little later than Colin Kafka and Stonehenge. It was called the Hare and Hounds. Which were we? I wondered. Neither. We were just fucking idiots.

They were halfway through their pints. I furled my wet umbrella. They looked vaguely pleased to see me. I doubted that I was capable of looking pleased to see anything. Let alone them. Yeah, well. I threw them a sneer and went over to the bar. I returned with a pint of my own and sat down heavily on a stool.

"Do you have the . . . ?" asked Kafka.

I murmured an agreement. Of course I had them. I tapped my coat pocket, just so that he didn't ask me again. Stonehenge looked awkward. Not strictly his deal, I supposed. But things had changed. And we had to be ready for anything. Stonehenge may have looked uncomfortable, but he kept his mouth shut. Which meant he knew the score. I wondered just how uncomfortable he was going to look down in the tunnels. I wondered if he'd be able to keep his mouth shut when the squealing started. Or that hideous moaning. I remembered what Kafka had said about the tape recording. My name, in amongst the moaning. It didn't seem like a good omen. But then, nothing did.

The pub had big picture windows. They opened out over Charlcombe and all the way over more hills than I could be bothered to look at. Stonehenge shuffled his chair over to give me a good look.

"Impressive view, hey, Valpolicella?" he said.

"I'm not here to appreciate the stupid countryside. So. It gets dark at ten P.M. We've got six hours at least before they start their fucking monkey business. Are you certain that you didn't get tailed up here?"

"Absolutely sure. After your call we took extra care. Not that we wouldn't have anyway. We split up, took separate routes, met up as if by accident. Do you have any plans?"

I thought for a while. I drank fast. Smoked half a cigarette. "Yeah. I've got a plan. Like I said, we've got six hours before dark. We've got protection. We're all here. Except Barry, who is otherwise engaged. I say we get down there straight away."

Kafka put his glass on the table. He took a deep breath. "Really? Now?"

"Really. Now," I said quietly.

Stonehenge wagged his head from side to side. "We should wait until it's dark."

"Why the hell should we wait until it's fucking dark?" I asked angrily. "When it's Sunday, when there's no one around, when we've got plenty of time? What is this? *Scooby-Doo?* What are you waiting for? A clap of thunder? Unearthly cackling? We should get a head start. Work out where we'll be in relation to this goddamn map of yours. Find the vats and blast them. What else are you planning? A late lunch, maybe?"

"He's fucking crazy, but he's right," insisted Kafka to Stonehenge. I was surprised. I'd tagged Kafka as reluctant. Maybe I'd been wrong.

"What's the point in sitting around up here? If we're going to have to do it, I'm all for starting it now. I don't want to hang around worrying, fretting, maybe deciding to fuck off. That's just bullshit. I reckon we should just get stuck in!"

"Yeah, come on, Stonehenge," I hissed, "what the fuck are you so frightened of? We've both been down there. You haven't. It's time to test your knowledge, time to test your nerve. I've got the shooters, you've got the map, and we've got the bollocks. *Let's get down there and kill some fucking pigs.*"

Stonehenge looked at us. He looked at me. Then he looked at Kafka. Then he sighed. Took a pull on his pint. He shuddered. He was trying to be cool, but it didn't wash. And he knew it. He didn't want to be involved in this any more than we did. And, like us, professional curiosity had got the better of him. Barry had contacted him. He'd contacted me. I'd contacted Kafka. Or had Kafka contacted me? I couldn't remember. It didn't seem important. And now here we all were, drinking beer but not tasting it, looking at a view but not seeing it, talking about something but not doing it. It had all collapsed on his head. He'd never really thought it was serious. It had all been historical research. Myth. Legend. And now all that stood between him and a sixty-foot journey underground to a subterranean world of sheer terror was approximately half a pint of beer. I was looking forward to seeing how he dealt with it.

"I, I really don't think . . . ."

He wasn't dealing with it very well. He was practically gibbering.

"You'll have a gun," I reminded him. I spoke quietly. People were having normal times around us, and I didn't want to disturb them. As I think I mentioned before, I'm a civilised kind of guy. "And there's some woods just over the road from here. We can practise. You'll be great, I can tell from the way you act so reluctant. People who are too keen are just a liability. If you're going to be effective, you need to be very calm. Very cool. Very collected. You're that sort, Stonehenge."

This time he had a vague glint in his eye. I'd excited him. He might even have believed me, at least for now. "Okay," he said, "maybe you're right. We go down now. Forget the target practice. I'll be fine. What was it that one of you said? Just point and click? We'll need all the ammunition we have. Let's not waste it. Right then. We check out the tunnels, find the chloroethylene vats and the altar, and wait." He looked at me. "And we kill those pigs. If they don't kill us first."

"Yeah, well," I said, clapping him on the shoulder. "Let's go."

CHAPTER 19

FUCKING HORRIBLE

We left the hill-top pub and found a footpath that led down towards Charlcombe. It was a steep path, down the side of a muddy field. The rain was continuous, and my umbrella was no good because I needed my arms to steady myself on the gradient. I threw it onto the wet grass. An umbrella was no defence where I was going. We slid to a halt at the stile at the bottom of the field. The lane just below was deserted. A few hundred yards round the corner was the path that led further down the valley to the KHS dig. To the hole. The pit. Or whatever the hell it was.

I checked my watch again. It was just after 6 P.M. But getting dark. Unseasonable weather. The grey clouds shrouded the sun. It felt like it was later. Much later. The wind was picking up, the trees around us bowing to it, or to something. It was cold down in the valley. Much colder than it should have been. The gap in the hedge was further than I remembered. But it was there. We squeezed through, casually, as if we were three guys out for an afternoon walk after a few beers at the pub. Yeah, well. In the pouring rain it maybe didn't look so convincing. Kafka spoke first.

"There's a guy over there, just standing around by the tarpaulin."

He was right. Hundred percent right. A sentry, a guard, whatever. The guy hadn't noticed us yet. He was sheltering just under the tarp. We followed the footpath. We were going to have to do something about the security guard, or else we really were on a Sunday stroll. A stroll to nowhere. We walked over a ridge until we were out of sight.

"What the fuck is he doing there?" said Kafka between his teeth.

"I said we should wait until dark!" said Stonehenge.

I turned round and faced the two of them. "Shut up. No unnecessary discussion, okay? We're here to do a job. No talking unless it's vital. No fucking argument. *Get it?*"

They both nodded. That was good. I didn't want to get into any bullshit with Stonehenge when we had a herd of demonic pigs chasing us.

"Now. There's one guard. One guard that we've seen. There may be more. Okay. There have never been guards before, so they must know that we've been nosing around. Why are we here? We're here to prevent a murder. At least."

"At the very least," murmured Stonehenge.

"Okay," said Kafka, "let's scout the site. If that bloke's the only guard, we deal with him. Knock the fucker out. But we don't harm him unnecessarily. I know what security guards get paid. Not enough to get dead for. But we tie him up, right?"

"Yeah, well," I added, "he'd better be tied up good. The way I see it, we're going to be in trouble whatever happens. But the more time we have, the better."

Me and Stonehenge laid low under cover of the ridge while Kafka took a recce. He was back inside ten minutes. I'd hardly started on my second cigarette.

"He's the only one. As far as I can tell."

"How far's that?" I asked. "Are there any more guards under the tarp?"

"None. I got round to the back of the dig. Nobody. But there's no way we can get in there without him noticing. We're going to have to deal with him. Martin?"

I growled. I dislike violence, but I mind it less when it's unavoidable. And I don't mind it at all when it's going to stop me being arrested for murder. And brutal, savage, twisted murder at that.

I ambled across the field in the general direction of the guard. Innocent. Taking an interest in the trees, the hills, the view. Stopping occasionally to check the view down across the eastern fringes of the city, over to the hills beyond. Oh, very beautiful. Veiled in rain, but nice all the same, right? Oh, for sure. The guard started taking notice of me when I was about two hundred yards from him. I waved. He didn't wave back. I started walking towards him with a certain amount of purpose. Say, what's that big blue tarpaulin all about? Maybe that guy standing by it can tell me. Hey, I'm a happy, outdoors kind of guy. But I wasn't in a hurry. I stopped here and there, examining trees or whatever. It was slow, but I reached him in the end.

"Hello there," I said brightly, "the rain's not so bad once you're out in it, is it?"

"Fucking horrible."

I punched him hard in the gut and he toppled. I sat on his chest. A guard off his guard. Easy. I pinned his arms with my knees and held his windpipe. Kafka came hurrying over.

"Find some rope," I spat, "and gag the fucker."

Kafka did the necessary. Once the guard was trussed and silenced, I stood up. Then Stonehenge jogged over. This wasn't his scene. It wasn't my scene either. I wished I could have stayed in the Hare and Hounds, admiring the rain.

"Is he going to be okay?" asked Stonehenge, nodding towards the struggling guard.

"Probably more okay than we're going to be," I replied. "Why the fuck are you bothered? Shall we descend to the underworld?"

I pointed out the CCTV cameras, and we picked our way across the muddy planks to the centre of the dig. It got drier as we walked towards the hole. Kafka and Stonehenge looked eerie in the blue light that came through the tarp. I guess I did, too. It was as dry as I remembered around the hole. The ladder was still there. And the winch. And the props. It was only the second time I'd seen it in the light, if that's what you could call it under the blue tarpaulin. About eight feet diameter. And dark, down there. Very dark.

"The first time I went down there," I said quietly, turning to Kafka, "it was the same diameter all the way down. No wider at the bottom than it is here. The next time I went down—with you—it was twenty or thirty feet in diameter at the bottom. Twenty-four hours later."

Kafka looked at me. A stern expression. Not doubting, but, well, unsure. I continued.

"You know as well as I do that nothing about this hole is . . . right. It's wrong. In every way. I don't know why or how, but these tunnels play with us. With our minds. You got a different tape recording than what we heard. I got a different hole than I expected. So, how about this. We all study Stonehenge's map. We decide what to do. We work out a left, right, left, right, right, left, or whatever. We do not change our minds. Does that sound like a good idea? Because it fucking well better."

"Clear," said Kafka.

"Look," said Stonehenge, "I'm not used to making everything up as I go along, but it seems that we have no choice. If we're to stop Them, we have to be very, very careful. We *have* to know what we're doing."

Wow. This was Stonehenge the prof talking. I was almost impressed. It looked like he'd got over his fear, his concern, or whatever it was. I almost missed his unique line in taking twice as long as he needed to say anything at all.

"The main trouble is that we're about a mile north of the chloroethylene vats. Well, slightly to the northeast. Due south of here is the Circus, which is really where we need to be. That is the hub of the tunnel system. The thing is, I'm certain that the Circus cavern is extremely well guarded. Trying to get into it would be suicide. And a very unpleasant suicide. Here, look at the map."

The map was bad news. To me it looked like a mess. An incomprehensible mess.

"Are you sure that's a map?"

"Of course it's a map! Look! Here's the Circus. Here's the three tunnels radiating out from it. The northern tunnel leads directly to where we are. To Charlcombe."

Stonehenge was stabbing his finger on the piece of paper he was calling a map, but it took me a couple of minutes to see what he meant. It wasn't like any sort of map I'd ever seen. More like a diagram of somebody's memories. Even more like something you'd find scrawled on the floor in a building for people who might need upholstered walls. Whatever. But it made sense, after a while.

"I'm really fucking worried about the pigs," said Kafka.

"I'm really fucking worried about the pigs, too," I muttered, still staring at the map.

"Shoot the leading pig," announced Stonehenge. "That should frighten the rest. I don't know how long for. I don't know if these pigs are tribal. If they have a hierarchy. But I imagine that they do. All the legends concerning the Fleet Pigs talk of a queen. If there is a queen, then it follows that there should be tribal leaders."

"You imagine. *If.* Then it follows. You're very good, Stonehenge. I'm very, very glad that we've got you with us. Tell you what, when we get face to face with Queen Pig, you can do the diplomatic bit, okay?"

I ground my cigarette out with my shoe. Stonehenge hadn't made me any less worried about the pigs. I glanced at Kafka. He didn't look particularly uplifted either. But the top of the ladder was still here. The rungs got harder to see as they were swallowed by that yawning darkness.

"What's that smell?" asked Stonehenge. He swung his face around. But we knew where it came from. Even if we didn't know what it was.

"It's from the pit," said Kafka simply. "It comes in waves. It can get pretty intense down at the bottom. And worse in the tunnels, because there's no way out."

This was stupid. We were standing around doing nothing, scaring the crap out of ourselves. Pathetic. The other two carried on talking, but I didn't listen. I walked closer to the hole and stared down into it. It was like a well full of ink. Black ink, the darkest, most viscous, velvety ink I could have imagined. And as I stood there, a gasp of sulphur retched from its depths. The odour washed over me. I didn't care about that any more. I didn't really care about anything any more. I was ready to go down.

CHAPTER 20

DON'T FUCKING PANIC

We worked out a route from the map. Committed it to memory. Or tried to. I went down first. Stonehenge next. Then Kafka. I could almost taste the darkness after only about five rungs. I had a sudden crisis of confidence. Luckily it was a very quick one. I didn't have time to stop climbing, or anything like that. Step after step. Once Stonehenge lowered himself into the hole, it got really dark. His bulk blocked out the blue light. I kept climbing down. Eyes open or shut, it made no difference. A wave of sulphur gusted gently over me. More than once. It was like the tunnels were—breathing, or something.

No one said anything the whole way down. It was a long trip. Took a long time. I thought about whistling, but I couldn't remember a tune. I got the same feeling as ever, of being alone in the universe. A lonely universe. An endless tube, spinning and spinning in the emptiness. It got so I couldn't tell if I was climbing up or down. I was just climbing. I thought about all this stuff for a while. Passed the time. After that I started counting rungs, but then I forgot whether I was counting with my left hand or my left foot. I tried to work that out, but I didn't get anywhere. Then I started wondering whether I was going down or up again.

Okay. I don't want to bore you as much as I got bored. That would be horrible. Yeah, well.

It wasn't any more fun at the bottom, but I felt a shudder of gratitude at being able to stop climbing. I had been going downward after all. I stepped away from the ladder as Stonehenge and then Kafka reached the end of it. I waited for a while as we got our breath back. Then I reached inside my pocket for my flashlight.

Well, we were in a chamber. Okay. But it wasn't the same chamber that me and Kafka had found less than twenty-four hours ago. It was bigger. Much bigger. Thirty feet in diameter? Forty? I didn't care. It wasn't relevant. I heard Kafka gasp. Or maybe it was me. I swept the beam around the walls of the chamber. Still three tunnels. Still the weird bell-jar shape, like being in some kind of dome. Still mud walls. Still flagstones on the floor.

"What is this place?" breathed Stonehenge. He wasn't asking us. He was just wondering out loud to himself.

"Which tunnel was it?" asked Kafka.

I kept the beam moving because I couldn't think of anything to say. Then I thought of something.

"I don't know," I muttered.

"Good job that I brought this then," said Stonehenge, fumbling in his pockets. He pulled out a compass. "We need to go due south. Oh. Oh no."

"What is it?" asked Kafka.

"Take a look at this," Stonehenge grunted bitterly.

We crowded round. The little needle on the compass was spinning wildly, sporadically swinging one way then the next.

"It must be the iron content in the rock down here . . . ." Stonehenge was trying to rationalise something that was three dozen stops past Barking. Iron content? Oh, for sure. That'll be it. I guess the fact that the chamber had enlarged itself had one of those logical, scientific-type explanations, too.

"Put your goddamn toy away," I said. "And tell me what you think will happen if we try firing a gun. Maybe the lead content in the rocks will fuck the bullets up. No, actually, don't bother trying to think of something. I couldn't bear it. Hey, Colin. Have you got any idea—any idea at all—which way we went last night?"

He trailed his eyes around the walls of the chamber. Shook his head.

"Wait a minute," said Stonehenge. "Take a look at the bottom of the ladder. That's our reference point. I'm guessing, but I think we climbed down facing roughly south. So if we take that tunnel . . . there, it should be the right one."

I shot him a grudgingly admiring glance.

"Okay. I'll go first, then you, Stonehenge, then Colin. A couple of things. No random flashlight use. No unnecessary talking. And if you need to fire a gun, make sure you know exactly what you're pointing at. What I'm saying is, make sure it's not me. Clear?"

They nodded.

"Okay. Colin, here's yours." I handed him a gun.

"And Stonehenge? Here's yours. This is the safety. Keep it pressed down. Flick it up when you need to, if you need to. Keep your arm steady when you aim and if you fire. Make sure you've got a clear shot. Squeeze the trigger, don't pull it. Just remember: steady, steady, steady. Don't fucking panic. If your head's panicking, make sure your arm's cool. Right? Steady. Squeeze. And only—absolutely only—when you have to, when there's no other thing you can do. Okay?"

Stonehenge took the pistol. He looked at it a little apprehensively. That was okay. Apprehensively is the only way to look at gun, the way I figure it.

I took another look around the chamber. Water dripped constantly from above. It wasn't homely, but the tunnels, I knew, were worse. Much worse. It was cold. Three people against a global conspiracy. Flesh-eating pigs. Sacrifice. Yeah, well. I pointed my flashlight towards the tunnel that we had to assume was the right one. And I started walking towards it.

At the entrance to the tunnel I stopped. I turned around. Kafka and Stonehenge were whispering to each other.

"Come on then," I said. They stopped conferring and followed me over. They didn't look too happy. I wasn't grinning myself.

"Ready?" They looked at each other, then at me. Kafka made a grunting affirmative sound. Stonehenge nodded slightly. "Okay. Let's go," I said, with an authority I didn't feel. I snapped off the flash. We walked forward, into the darkness.

One thing hadn't changed since last night. Walking into the tunnel was like walking into fog. Thick, dense fog. I held my gun in one hand, and with the other trailed my fingers along the wet, slimy wall. I could hear Stonehenge and Kafka's footsteps behind me, but they were a little muffled. I couldn't hear anything else, apart from an intermittent dripping. There was nothing else. Yet.

The smell of sulphur was stronger than in the chamber, but I was expecting that. Stonehenge gagged a few times. But he'd be okay. He'd better be. I tried closing my eyes. No difference. Opened them. No difference. I wasn't about to try that too often, or else I wouldn't know whether they were open or shut. Even if I couldn't see anything, I wanted the option to be there. What was I looking for? Oh yeah. Vats of dry-cleaning fluid. Naturally. And pigs. Whatever. We had stuff to do. What was the order of importance? Destroy the vats. Get Barry out. Rescue the sacrificial victim. Right. A breeze. Piece of cake.

Then I heard something. Or I thought I heard something. Maybe it was Kafka. I stopped dead. I said, "Sshh." Kafka and Stonehenge stopped, too.

"What did you say?" I whispered back to Kafka.

"Nothing. What did you say?" he whispered back.

"I didn't say anything either."

We stood in silence for a long time. Or a short time. I couldn't tell. But I hadn't been wrong. There was a sound, and it wasn't our footsteps, and it wasn't dripping water. As far as I could tell it was a sort of thrumming, throbbing sound. Like something with a very deep voice muttering something unimaginably obscene, very slowly. Not quite regularly. Very, very distant. As if it was very loud, though. As if it was coming through layers of rock and clay, faintly echoing along the maze of tunnels. Through the catacombs. It wasn't a reassuring sound. I might have said something to that effect. I don't know.

I remember Kafka swearing softly, and a faint worried noise coming from Stonehenge. I took my hand from the wall and grabbed for one of my whiskey bottles. Then I put my gun in my pocket and unscrewed the bottle cap. I took a big swallow. I passed it back, and I heard Kafka, then Stonehenge taking similarly large gulps. The bottle came back. I had another swig, put the cap back on, and slid it back in my pocket. I took my gun out again. We walked on.

It wasn't much further on when the wall wasn't there under my fingertips. I halted. Kafka stumbled into my back, then I felt a lurch as Stonehenge bumped into him. We steadied ourselves.

"Okay," I whispered, "I'm going to turn my flashlight on. Just me. The wall isn't there any more. I think it's where me and Colin found the first crossroads last night. But I'm going to check." I flicked the switch. The light was gloomy and yellowish, not bright at all. But it was enough. We were in a cavern. It was enormous. Horribly enormous. Slowly I moved the beam of the flash around. The ground was level, paved with flagstones, but there was enough of it to—to, I don't know—have a football match? A military parade? For all the damned in hell to park their fucking cars? It was huge. Immense. My flashlight barely found the edges of it.

"This wasn't here last night, Stonehenge," I whispered. "If we're in the same tunnel as last night. Big if. But we definitely went south last night. Because of where we got out. And we're pretty clear that we're going south now. Fact is, I've never seen this before. But then the chamber at the bottom of the hole wasn't there last night either, not like it is tonight. So, that leads me to a conclusion. I don't like it, but I don't like anything that's happened in the last couple of days. These tunnels change. They change shape."

"We've got to be in another tunnel," said Kafka. "They can't change shape. They just . . . they just *can't!*"

"They just can. They just do. And as long as we stay alive, we're going to have to deal with it. Okay. We're going to keep straight ahead. I'll keep the flashlight on."

"Just a moment," said Stonehenge insistently. "If you're right—and I'm assuming that you are—how do we know if we can get back? How do we know if we can get out?"

"Good question. I was wondering that myself. I didn't get as far as finding an answer. Sorry. But I don't think there is one. Any other questions? Not that I'll have any answers to them, either, but you might like to ask them anyway."

There was silence.

"Okay. Straight on, I think."

We trudged across the cavern floor. Flagstones stretched out in all directions. I couldn't tell how high the ceiling was, because the beam didn't reach that far. The space didn't feel huge. The cloying atmosphere saw to that. It looked immense, but it felt claustrophobic. After a long time we reached the wall at the opposite side.

As usual, it was clay, with rocks poking out all over the place, and wetness glistening everywhere. I couldn't figure out how it had been made. There was no sign of what had been used to hollow it out. Just little, soft-looking ridges. It was like the inside of a mouth. There was an opening in the wall, which went pretty much in the direction we'd been heading. It looked a little small. A little low. We'd have to stoop. Which meant that it would be hard to see straight ahead. It would be hard to see what was in front of us, especially if I turned my flashlight off. I briefly thought about the pigs. We'd have to kneel to get a clear shot. There was barely enough room for two of us to fire. If Stonehenge panicked and let fly, then me or Kafka would get a bullet in the back of the head. It looked too cosy. Too intimate. Too intimate for three frightened men with loaded guns.

"Looks like we got a problem," I said. "That's a very little tunnel. Not much room for anything but scurrying along with our heads bent, watching the flagstones. Any ideas? Anyone?"

"Can you hear something?" said Kafka, quickly. Urgently.

"What?" asked Stonehenge.

"*Sshh!*"

Kafka was right. It was hard to hear because it sounded so far away. But I'd heard it before. Those blind, hairless, hungry children. The pigs. We could hear the pigs. I couldn't tell how far off they were. But however far that was, it wasn't as far away as when we couldn't hear them at all. Which could only mean one thing. They were getting nearer.

"What is that?" murmured Stonehenge.

"It's the pigs, Stonehenge. The Fleet Pigs. The *flesh-eating* Fleet Pigs. Bladud's best friends. Sound like sweet little things, don't they? Yeah. For sure. Whatever. It occurs to me that we're maybe too visible here in this fucking cavern. Let's go!"

We threw ourselves into the tunnel. It was cramped, but not too bad. We pelted along, the beam from my flashlight weaving and jittering about in front. The flagstones were wetter down here, slick with algae or mould or something. I couldn't tell colours. Everything was yellow or black. The colours of plague and death. And the smell was disgusting. It wasn't just sulphur any more. It was beyond foul, the smell of rain-rotted rats and wet, tacky dead skin, of putrefying corpses and fetid ooze seeping from countless crushed bodies, the smell of the hum of thousands upon thousands of flies feeding and egg-laying in the mounds of decaying flesh, the stench of an overfull oubliette, of cramped prisoners forgotten for months in some hellish dungeon . . . .

The next thing I knew, I was being pulled up by my arm. Kafka was saying something to me, but I couldn't hear it. There was a light in my eyes. I couldn't see. I tried to brush it away. I was in some sort of thick silence. Hands grabbed at me, pulled me upright, slammed me against the cold wall.

"Valpolicella! *Valpolicella!*"

I murmured something. I don't remember what it was. Shapes started to get more distinctive. Kafka and Stonehenge. They were staring at me with some kind of urgency. They were talking. Asking me stuff.

"Get that light out of my face," I think I said. I probably said that, because it went away. I was very wet. But I was standing. Or at least, I was being held up in a standing position. The tunnel was much wider and higher here; there was room to stand up. I looked around. You could get a truck through here.

But something else was going on. After the scuffle of getting me upright, shouting at me or whatever, Kafka and Stonehenge had gone motionless. The three of us were frozen like dead men. I flicked my eyes right, left, up, down. Nothing.

"What is it?" I said, very quietly. There was no answer, but Kafka's gaze met mine. With a couple of tiny movements, he jerked his head in the direction we were heading and pointed to his ear. I got the message. I listened, carefully. There was a voice. Distorted and broken, as if it was coming through something much denser and more evil than fog. I couldn't tell what it was saying for a little while. And then it started to form itself into thickly spoken, drooling words. It was some foreign-sounding stuff. I couldn't figure out what it might be. But it was like what Kafka had said that morning, in the café, a million years ago. '*Memvola sintrompo. Kontentiga morto.*' Over and over. But there were two words that I recognised, sandwiched in between the gibberish. '*Martin*' and '*Valpolicella.*' In between all of it was some terrible screaming—but still, it was distant. It was from very far away. Not round the next corner. To be honest, it didn't sound exactly as if it was in any normal sort of frequency. From any normal kind of world. And I couldn't hear the pigs.

"That's a pretty goddamn unpleasant kind of noise," I said, my voice still low, "but I can't hear the Fleet Pigs any more. We've got to carry on. What we're hearing is probably, um, probably a tape recording." Was I really saying this? A tape recording? "Yeah, that's what it is. A tape recording from last night is what it is, right? Kafka, isn't it just what you got on the tape last night? Am I right or am I right?"

Kafka slowly shook his head. "It's not the same. Not the same at all," he said. "It's pretty much the same words, but it's more—frenzied."

"Which means that They're down here already," muttered Stonehenge. "They're preparing, already. They will have Their victim by now. Who will be terrified out of his or her wits—held in an iron cage while the altar preparations are made. I had no idea that They would be here so early."

I swung my arm up. It felt too heavy. I took in the time. 8 P.M. Already? Yeah, well. I couldn't be sure, not after what had happened to Stonehenge's compass. But I figured that my watch had to be at least mostly right. Not Greenwich Mean Time, perhaps. But Valpolicella Mean Time. And that had to be enough for now.

"It makes no difference. There's nothing else we can do. We've got to keep going," I said. In that dim, fogged yellow light it was hard to tell how Kafka and Stonehenge felt. They looked like weird shadow devils in the dim amber fog. I leant back against the wall and dragged out the whiskey bottle. I had a hard swallow. Then another. I passed the bottle. It came back empty.

I held the neck in my hand and smashed it against the wall. Now I had another weapon. Not as technologically advanced as a gun, but anyway. I tested one of the gleaming glass points on my finger. It was very, very sharp. It would be helpful. But even though I knew I was going to have to use it, I still hoped that I wouldn't need to. Deceptive thinking. Dangerous thinking. I took a deep breath, and told myself to remember how to fight. Maximum violence, instantly. Don't think. Just fight. Just . . . fight.

"Okay," said Kafka. "Okay. Let's move."

We all had our flashlights on now. Not that they made much impression on the tangible darkness that surrounded us. The flagstones were slimy and slippery with mould, and the walls and ceiling looked yellowy-orange. Or red. Ahead and behind was a darkness that no light could illuminate. Wetness dripped down on us as constantly as rain. We trudged forward. And downward. There was a definite slope to the tunnel. I had some crazy stuff running around in my head. Bad crazy stuff. I tried not to give it too much room. I kept it shut tight behind my teeth.

Nobody said anything for a while. The distant howling continued. It kept mentioning me. *Martin. Valpolicella. Martin.* I focused on the beam of wan light ahead of me. Black-stained flagstones. Red walls. My footsteps. My heart, beating. My breathing, hoarse. My courage, faltering. I kept on wondering what I'd done to deserve this. Whether I could have avoided it. Why in hell Karen had done this to me. How could she have done this to me? We'd been, I don't know, close or something. I wasn't an expert, but I'd thought we'd got on okay. Better than okay. In my unguarded moments I'd even wondered if I'd fallen in love with her.

But now I was so far below the earth's surface I didn't want to think about it too hard. Chased by flesh-eating pigs down a foul tunnel towards some fiend chanting my name when it wasn't screaming like an audio collage of every torture victim the world's ever known. Was it just opportunism on Karen's part? Okay, we need a culprit, say AFFA. Any ideas, anyone? Oh, I know, pipes up Karen.

It just didn't gel. The Karen I knew wasn't like that at all. She was—she was *nice*. She gave every appearance of liking me—a lot. Yeah, the sex had been great, but there was something else, too. She really seemed to care about me. But what the hell did I know?

"I'm not certain, but I think we must be approaching the area where the chloroethylene vats are housed. We've been walking for an hour at least. Keep an eye out for left-hand turnings," said Stonehenge from behind me.

"We find these vats, we make holes in them with bullets, right?" I asked him, without turning round.

"From a safe distance," he replied quietly, "chloroethylene is, erm, rather flammable. Very flammable, in fact. So I'm told."

I stopped. Stonehenge and Kafka stumbled into me. I was standing firm. I let them untangle themselves before I spoke.

"Very flammable? Stonehenge. Have you ever thought about what 'very flammable' might actually mean in a series of very small tunnels? Explosions need an outlet, Stonehenge. I'm beginning to think that you don't actually know what the *fuck* you're doing. And that *worries* me, to put it fucking mildly." I think I might have waved the broken bottle around a little, underneath Stonehenge's chin. Maybe I did, maybe I didn't. I don't remember.

"Valpolicella. Take it easy." He sounded a little worried. Yeah, well.

"How easy? So easy I don't care about being a part of the wreckage after I pump a few shells into a huge vat of very flammable dry-cleaning fluid?" This was boring me. I didn't need an argument, not now. Not down here. Not with . . . .

"Did anyone hear that?" asked Kafka.

His voice was flat. The contrast with our own voices was enough to make us stop bickering. We listened. I couldn't hear anything at first. But then it was clear. Squealing. The pigs were back. I could hear them. It was a terrifying sound. Could I hear their trotters on the wet flagstones as they thundered closer, or was I imagining it? I didn't think so. The squealing was getting louder, for sure. I was suddenly aware of everything—the water falling constantly from above, the black mould below, the soul-destroying depth and magnitude of the catacombs, the impossibility of any kind of escape . . . .

I hefted my gun. The sound of the pigs was getting louder, I was sure. They were coming for us. I didn't know if they'd smelt us or been set on us or what. It wasn't relevant. They were coming. *The Fleet Pigs were coming.*

"Get your fucking guns ready. Stonehenge? Flick off the safety. Remember, it's aiming that's the important thing. Steady, squeeze . . . okay?"

And that was all that I could say. There was no point in running along a tunnel with a prehistoric herd of man-eating pigs snapping at our heels. We were going to have to wait. We were going to have to wait for the pigs. They still sounded some distance away. Maybe they were having some kind of pig gathering in the cavern. Maybe they'd choose some other tunnel to cruise. I didn't know anything about a pig's sense of smell. But I knew that they had very, very big snouts. Good for unearthing food. And somehow, I didn't think it would take very long before they found us. And you know what? I wasn't wrong. I wasn't wrong at all.

It was obvious that the pigs sniffed out our tunnel. The squealing became amplified beyond my belief. It was deafening, a reverberating echo of hell that thundered along the tunnel and assaulted our ears. It was all we could do to hold our guns steady at the inky darkness that contained that demonic cacophony. I held my gun in one hand and my broken bottle in the other, trying desperately to hold both steady. The beam from Kafka's flashlight wavered around.

Nothing happened. Not just yet. Just the squealing, growing louder and louder, filling the tunnel and surging towards us like a wave of hideousness. Now we could hear their trotters thundering on the flagstones, dozens of them, closer and closer.

And now they were right in front of us, a heaving pale mass of snouts and broad backs. They were ghastly, with skins that looked like they'd been left too long in stagnant water.

I fired once, then twice. Kafka's gun roared in my ear, then Stonehenge's, again and again and again. At first I thought we hadn't even slowed them down—they came rushing on, a ghostly sinuous mass of hungry teeth and muscle. But two pigs had gone down, and the others seemed frightened. Maybe.

They came to a gradual, shuffling halt, sniffing the bodies of their dead, then eyeing us with slowly swaying heads, grunting and sniffing the sulphurous air that surrounded us. There must have been maybe a hundred of them. More, probably. I wasn't counting. I couldn't see the end of the herd. The tunnel was full of pigs, as far back as the feeble beam from my flashlight would penetrate. Their wet white skins filled me with dread. Their eyes were jet black, gleaming in the yellow light. They were big. I wasn't an expert, but they were big. I couldn't see their teeth. Their mouths were hidden under their great snouts, their nostrils contracting and dilating as they scented us. As they figured out whether or not they could take us.

I took a pace towards them. They didn't retreat an inch. So neither did I. I stood still. Then, very slowly, I lifted my gun. I aimed straight at the pig nearest to me. It stood perfectly still, glaring at me with its glistening black eyes. Its head waggled slightly from side to side, but the eyes never left me. I felt like I was frozen. I stood there, soaking wet, feet planted firmly apart, holding my broken bottle, holding my gun. Staring down the pig. I wanted it to back away. I wanted it to turn and trot away, with all its pig friends. But things weren't going to happen that way. I should have known. Maybe I did know. Maybe I was just kidding myself. Whatever. The pig came closer, so I shot it right between the eyes.

Big mistake.

Pandemonium. The herd went berserk. Crazy. With a rising, howling, squealing collective bellow of rage they charged us, the instant the pig I'd shot went down. Shots rang out all over the place, echoing ear-splittingly in the confined space. We were running, shooting, screaming with fear. Pigs were everywhere, running back, forward, turning amongst themselves, colliding with massive thumps as their flanks slammed into other pigs, into the walls, into us. I couldn't tell what was happening to Stonehenge and Kafka; my whole being was dedicated to self-preservation and I ran like I'd never run before. Two massive pigs seemed to want to catch me, knock me over, and consume me. And I went over, crashing up against another pig. I tried to keep upright but my legs were trapped in a heaving mass of flesh. In a horrible moment I moved in slow motion, my torso partly rotating, a scream wrenching itself from my throat, then I was falling forward over a pig's back, not wanting to let go of my gun, pulling the trigger, swinging the broken bottle wildly, feeling its jagged shards tearing into solid pig muscle, then it slipping out from my sweating hand—and I was on the ground.

Filthy trotters stabbed me all over. Mouths full of sharp teeth snapped at me. The pigs were stampeding. I rolled through slime, cold water, and mud towards the wall and tried to make myself as small a target as I could. I pulled my arms up over my head and clenched my eyes tight shut. I waited for this nightmare to pass. I didn't know if it would. But I thought it might. And that was my only hope. I tried to keep hold of it, but I guess I passed out. Then I didn't need to worry about anything.

I couldn't have been out for long. A minute? Maybe two. The side of my face was in a freezing cold puddle of slimy water. I was glad it was cold—firstly, it woke me up, and secondly, I knew it couldn't have been blood. I lifted my head out of the water, and shuffled my legs into a crouching position. Maybe the pigs had gone. It was quiet. No, it wasn't. There was a scratchy, flailing sound, and some half-assed squeals. Wounded pigs, I guessed.

And I could hear the faint echo of distant chanting. I couldn't see anything.

What I could feel was a whole lot of pain, all over. I was pain. It was pitch black. I hoped I still had my torch. I checked my pockets. Lucky. It was there. I noticed that my other hand was still gripping something. My gun. Also lucky. Some reflex had kept my hand clenched like a claw around it. I flicked the switch on the flash and swung the beam around slowly.

Fuck. What a mess. There was blood everywhere, and churned mud. About eight or nine pigs lay bleeding on the filthy flagstones. Most of them seemed to still be alive. Well, not very alive. But not very dead either. Some of them were threshing around and foaming at the mouth, blood and saliva all over their faces. There was pig shit everywhere. Their squeals sounded pathetic now, not frightening. The stench was fucking disgusting. But I wasn't about to start feeling sorry for them. And I wasn't about to waste any ammunition on putting them out of what looked like considerable misery. I struggled up to my feet, leaning against the wall for support. I swung the torch around some more.

No Stonehenge. No Kafka. I looked around for my broken whiskey bottle, then saw it stuck in the neck of a dead pig. I decided to leave it there. I searched my pockets for the other bottle and took a big drink. Then I had another. I put the bottle carefully back into my pocket. Now then. Where were Kafka and Stonehenge? Only one way to find out. I started walking. Gun in one hand. Flashlight in the other. Very pissed off.

I tried to figure out what might have happened. Maybe the other two had escaped up a side tunnel. I hadn't seen any yet, but that didn't mean there weren't any further on. I dreaded coming across a human body, lying maybe half-eaten in the muck and slime on the floor. What the fuck did these pigs do when they got it into their heads to eat someone? I didn't know. I reckoned that I'd had a lucky escape, what with blacking out and all. They must have missed me in the confusion of the stampede, when they didn't know what the hell was going on. A lucky break. Maybe things were starting to go my way. Yeah, well. That idea lasted about two seconds. If things were going my way I'd wake up in bed and this would all have been a nightmare. Some hope. Whatever. I just walked forward. Listening to that horrible chanting that just went on and on.

After a long time of nothing happening apart from water dripping on my head and a growing feeling of cold and hopelessness, I came to a crossroads. Maybe it was the one where the left-hand turning went to the spiral staircase that led up to the crypt. No good. I remembered the heavy coffin that me and Kafka had manhandled onto the trapdoor. No chance of escape that way. But I figured that I had to at least try to locate Kafka and Stonehenge. At least try. Give it a go. I swung the torch down the right-hand turning. There was something down there. Something huddled. Something human? I stepped carefully, slowly towards it. It didn't seem to be moving. I got close enough for the feeble beam from my flashlight to slide over the form. Human, yes. I moved closer, jiggled the beam. It was Kafka.

CHAPTER 21

EYES WIDE OPEN

"Colin!" I hissed, bending towards him. He didn't move. I grabbed his shoulder and shifted him over. His head lolled. His eyes were shut. He looked in bad shape.

"Colin!" No luck. I checked him for injuries. Nothing obvious. Nothing I could see, anyway. I pulled the other whiskey bottle from my pocket. I had a deep drink, then poured a generous slug over Kafka's face. It seemed to help. Muscles moved beneath his muddy skin. His mouth opened slightly. I poured a little more.

"What the fuck . . . ."

"Evening, Colin. Welcome back."

"What? Who . . . ? Martin . . . . Fucking hell, what happened? Shit, what is this stuff on my face?"

"Some of my whiskey. There's not much left, and what there is I'm going to drink." I drank it.

"What happened?" whimpered Kafka again.

"Pigs. The Fleet Pigs. That's what happened. Remember? Big herd of huge white pigs. They stampeded. All over us. We got split up. I got unconscious. Some of the pigs got dead, but not many. I woke up in a pool of slime. Went looking for you. Wasted some whiskey on your ugly mug. And here we are. Any idea what happened to Stonehenge?"

Kafka wiped his face. It was streaked with whiskey-diluted mud. But no blood. He raised himself up on his elbows. Closed his eyes. Opened them again.

"I . . . I'm not sure. Let me think . . . . Yeah, the pigs. We lost you. Had to run, had to get away from them. They chased us. We couldn't shoot, couldn't turn round, running, no time. Stonehenge, he, he was in front of me . . . I don't know where . . . ." Kafka sat up straight, patted himself all over. He looked wildly around the floor. "My gun. It's gone!"

"Shit. That's not good. Not any of it. Can you stand up?"

"Yeah, I think so."

I helped him get up. He seemed a little wobbly, but otherwise okay.

"This isn't going too well," I said. "Chanting. Pigs. One gun lost. No Stonehenge. And it must be getting late." I glanced at my watch. 11 P.M. It was late. 11 P.M.? How? But there it was, on the dial. Unless my watch was messing me around. Unless this place was messing my watch around. Whatever. I passed my gun to Kafka, held my flashlight between my teeth, and unstrapped the damn thing from my wrist. Dangled it between my finger and thumb. Dropped it. Ground it between my heel and the flagstones. Shone the flashlight on the broken remains.

"Stupid fucking watch has been nothing but trouble. Might have missed some of those meetings without it. I might not have ended up in this stinking sewer."

"But you have ended up here. Almost as if you'd had *no choice*."

The voice came from behind me. I nearly let out a yelp of surprise. Maybe I did. I wheeled round and saw Stonehenge.

"Fuck! Stonehenge! You scared the shit out of me!"

Stonehenge just stood there.

"Where the hell have you been? Are you okay?" I asked. But there was a slight tension in my forehead. An involuntary quizzical look was forming on my face. Stonehenge had his gun. He had it pointed at me. Joke? I didn't think so. My brain did a few somersaults, a couple of cartwheels, before it stopped fucking about and started working for a living. I accelerated through the last few days. Rewind. Fast forward. Looking for something— anything—that could explain what the hell Stonehenge was doing. Mind control. What had he told us about mind control? That AFFA had worked out how to do it? Shit, I wished that I'd paid a bit more attention.

"Stonehenge. AFFA are messing with your head. They're controlling your mind. Can you hear me? Do you understand? Do you understand?" I stared at him. A hard stare. I put everything I had into it. All my energy, out through my eyes. No dice.

"I am under the control of AFFA." He spoke haltingly, as if he'd been programmed. Oh, shit. I tried again.

"Stonehenge! It's me, Martin Valpolicella. Think! We came down the hole. We were chased by the Fleet Pigs. We got split up. Wake up, Stonehenge!"

He was still standing there, pointing the gun at me. Staring straight at me. Expressionless. This wasn't going too well.

"Ah, come on! Stonehenge, for fuck's sake! Don't you remember? Meeting in the Old Green Tree? My office? You told me about this, you told me about AFFA, you told me and Kafka that they used mind control! Listen to me! AFFA are controlling your mind! Yours, Stonehenge! Do you understand? Do you?"

"I am under the control of AFFA. AFFA are controlling my mind. I will do what They tell me."

I heard a sound behind me. I spun back round to face Kafka. He was standing straight up. He wasn't leaning, half-exhausted, against the wall any more. That in itself didn't bother me. What bothered me was the barrel of the gun I'd handed to him pointed straight at my stomach.

"I am under the control of AFFA," he said, mechanically. "AFFA are telling me that Martin Valpolicella is a fucking gullible prick . . . ." He dissolved into giggles, but the gun didn't waver. He stopped giggling. And looked at me with scorn. Spoke in his normal voice.

"You fucking gullible prick. You walked right into it, didn't you? Walked right in, eyes wide open. We didn't even need to offer you any money. Not one penny. Oh, dear me. Dearie me."

"What the . . . ." I felt something poking the small of my back. Something that was probably—no, definitely—Stonehenge's gun. Then I heard his voice, very close, very quiet.

"You've no idea how much fun this has been, Valpolicella. So much fun. It's been extremely difficult to keep a straight face. You behaving like the big man. Thinking that you were in control. Wonderful. It's added to the excitement quite a bit. Make sure he hasn't got any weapons, Colin."

Kafka frisked me. There was nothing to find. He took my flashlight. I eyed the empty whiskey bottle I'd left on the flagstones. Maybe . . . . I stopped eyeing it. Too late. Kafka saw where I was looking, tutted, and kicked it far down the tunnel. I heard it smash, far away.

"Good, weren't we?" said Stonehenge. "You don't need to answer that. If we hadn't been, you wouldn't be here. You'd have smelt a rat. Or a pig." He made some kind of laughing sound.

"Did you like our pigs? You don't need to answer that either. Pigs are very intelligent creatures. Though our pigs aren't quite—normal, they're very well trained. They can recognise faces, voices. They respond to simple commands. In that, they're very like dogs. Cleverer. Once you went over, we told them to leave you alone. We need you, you see. You're very important. Vital, even."

I just looked at him. Part of me didn't believe what I was hearing. But most of me did. There were a lot of questions I wanted to ask. More importantly, I wanted to get out. Out of these catacombs. Out of this city. Just—out. Far away. But that didn't seem very likely. Stonehenge, or whoever he was, and Kafka had the guns. I'd been played for a sucker. Yeah, well. I *was* a sucker. I'd known that this whole business was way out of my league. I'd known that for a while. But I'd still gone along with it.

"Let's get moving. It's nearly time," growled Stonehenge. "Come on, Valpolicella. Move it. Shift."

Stonehenge shoved me forward. Kafka led the way. The bastard knew where he was going, that was for sure. I lost track of the lefts and the rights. After ten minutes I'd completely lost whatever sense of direction I might have had. The tunnels seemed endless. The chanting was still audible. *Memvola sintrompo, memvola sintrompo, kontentiga morto, kontentiga morto.* Then my name, over and over. Then the gobbledegook again. Over and over. I couldn't tell if it was getting louder. It still sounded a long way off. But I figured it was louder than when I'd first heard it. I figured we were going towards it. There was that, there was the trudging of our feet on the slimy flagstones, the constant dripping of water from the roof. Water was running down the walls in glistening rivulets. I had plenty of time to reflect on my situation. Even if I hadn't got two fucking double-dealing bastards with guns keeping me moving in the direction they wanted, I couldn't have got out of this labyrinth. Whatever I did I was fucked. No weapon. No idea where I was. There was nothing to do but think, and even that was futile. Why the hell hadn't I seen this coming? Okay. I tried to run through what had happened. The note, first of all. I should have chucked it in the bin. Burnt it. Anything.

But I hadn't. Next, the e-mail from *valpolicellaneedtoknowthis*. Yeah. Or somebody needs Valpolicella. Then I'd met that girl actor. Then what? Charlcombe. The hole. Meeting Stonehenge in the Old Green Tree. Kafka. I remembered. I hadn't contacted Kafka. It'd been him that contacted me. That's what it had all been. People contacting me. But in the most esoteric ways. I couldn't fault their technique. They'd wanted to draw me in. They'd wanted me to believe, and I had. Shit. Okay. That much was clear. But what about the chamber at the bottom of the hole? What about the disgusting variety of darkness they had down here? The pigs? Those fucking things weren't normal porkers. No way.

"Hey, Stonehenge," I said.

"What?"

"How much is true? How much of what you told me is true?"

"Most of it, Valpolicella," he said from behind me. We trudged on.

"Okay, so most of it. What isn't?"

"A couple of things. It's not true that Karen is one of Us. And it's not true that Barry is going to wield the sacrificial weapon."

"Karen's not . . . *you fucking bastards!*"

I stopped. "You . . . you . . . ." I couldn't speak. I couldn't believe the betrayal—my betrayal—of Karen. I was filled with hatred. For myself. A few lies down the line and I was ready to believe fucking anything. I was ready to believe the woman who meant more to me than anyone—*anyone*—ever before, was some demonic priestess in a brutal cabal of murdering egomaniacs. Evidently, I would believe *anything*. It didn't take much to convince me of the most outlandish craziness. Somehow that wasn't so bad, believing stuff that my eyes showed me. But to believe this—this—stuff—about Karen . . . .

Fuck, I deserved it all. I deserved everything they could throw at me. I wished they hadn't called those fucking pigs off. Better to be eaten alive by mutant pigs than to be me.

"Get a move on." That was Kafka. He sounded impatient. Maybe he looked impatient. I couldn't tell. It was pretty dark, and there was some stuff in my eyes that made everything blurry. I shuffled onwards. Whatever was going to happen, I was condemned. By myself.

"Everything—all that stuff about mind control and whatever—is true?"

"Yes."

We walked and walked. I was a husk. My feet trod onwards, but they weren't anything to do with me. The chanting went on. I heard my name repeated, droning into my head. I'd have wanted the earth to swallow me up if it hadn't done it already. I was in hell.

"That chanting," I muttered. "What's it saying?"

"*Memvola sintrompo.* It means '*self-willed self-deception.*' That's you, Valpolicella. You were chosen. But, you know, you could have walked away. You chose this. They're chanting about you. You'll see."

"But—but everyone said I was going to be arrested for murder!"

Stonehenge just laughed. "Like I said, you'll see."

That seemed to be the end of the conversation. Self-willed self-deception? Yeah, well. I couldn't argue with that. I didn't want to. It was true. The chanting was definitely louder now. I kept stumbling. They kept shoving me onwards. I'd lost any kind of will or determination. All sense of time was gone. Everything was eternal. This was no time and every time. Maybe I'd been here forever, marching down these sloping flagstones, deeper and deeper into the ground. The muddy water dripped on me. Hell. Hell. Hell.

There was light ahead. Kafka was silhouetted against it. Greenish, bluish light, with a kind of flickering to it. The chanting was very loud now, and echoing. Kafka stopped and turned towards me. The light glowed like a mouldering halo around him.

"This is it, Valpolicella. Showtime. You ready?"

I might have nodded. I might have just stood there. I don't remember.

"Okay. It's your big moment. Come on."

The chanting suddenly stopped. I was led further. There was more of the light. Suddenly there was no more tunnel. Kafka stepped out of the way and I stood, blinking, trying to see what was in front of me. I was in a huge chamber. There was a stink of something clean and sweet, a nastily pungent odour. There were people in the chamber. People. Lots of them. Looking at me. The chamber was immense, shaped like the one under Charlcombe. Round the walls, fixed to the rock, were banks of flickering TV monitors, hundreds of them, ranged all the way around the vastness of the chambers. All showing CCTV footage from the city above, or scanning through thousands of faces, scanning, scanning . . . until they stopped. On my face. My face, at different times, in different places. But all me. All me.

I stopped looking at the monitors. Evenly spaced around the cavernous chamber were five huge glass vats filled with fluid, lit from beneath, with millions of tiny bubbles rising through them. That was the chloroethylene, I guessed. I looked at the people.

Oh, fuck. There were several I didn't recognise. But among them were Mario Murnau and Robinson from the CCTV control room. And the smartly dressed thugs who'd driven me out to the motorway and kicked my head in. The creeps Kafka had been interviewing in the Lud Club. The security guard we'd left trussed up at the edge of the Charlcombe dig. But not just *one* of them. *More* than one. It was too horrible. But there were *two* Murnaus. *Two* Robinsons. *Two* security guards. Two. Two of all of them. Identical twins? Not a fucking chance. These bastards were fucking cloned.

And facing me, glaring but grinning sadistically—Barry Eliot. The clones were in a circle around something in the centre of the chamber. Stonehenge's gun prodded at my back. I took a few steps forward, and the circle parted. The people on either side of Barry moved away from him. There was something behind him, but he obscured it.

"Welcome," he said. His voice echoed in the silence. None of the other mutant maniacs said a word. And then he moved away so I could see what was behind him. An altar, dead centre, underneath the highest point of the chamber. It was deeply carved with some pretty repellent stuff. Twisted limbs. Demonic faces. It looked very old, and very, very evil. Strapped down to it, bound and gagged, was Karen.

CHAPTER 22

ALIVE WITH CORRUPTION

My powers of recollection aren't a top-class operation at the best of times, but exactly what happened next is nowhere to be found in my memory. I think I may have freaked out a little. Called some people some names. Made some sort of violent attempt to hurt people. Like I say, it's all kind of vague. Whatever happened ended up with me being restrained from doing whatever it was I wanted to do.

The only thing I knew was that Karen was straining against the straps that held her down and I was straining against the arms that held me back. Some of the people made some of their own violent attempts to hurt me, but I didn't notice. I was more angry about my stupid, stupid belief in their lies than anything else. They'd played me for a sucker, and they'd fed me lies. And I'd believed them. I'd believed them.

I made a desperate attempt to break the grasp of whoever it was that was holding me. I wanted to get to Karen. But there were too many of them. I felt like a wild beast, shackled and brought down. I was kneeling on the flagstones, my arms held halfway up my back. They could do anything they liked. Anything. I was helpless. And very, very unhappy. But this wasn't the time to complain. Yeah, well.

Kafka and Stonehenge grabbed me around my upper arms. Murnau and Robinson helped them in some way. All of them were laughing. Fuck it, I didn't see anything funny about anything. I guess that's how the butt of any joke feels. They dragged me out of the chamber into some other room. The decor didn't surprise me. Rock and clay walls, flagstone floor, mould, damp. No doors or exits apart from the one I'd been dragged through. No escape. Nothing new there.

They put me in some kind of stone chair with straps that did up tight. They left the room. Still having a laugh. The situation was hilarious. Oh, for sure. Then Barry came in.

Barry was a fat-faced, thick-lipped, well-fed looking bastard. Facial muscles crunched over his eyebrows. He had a terse mouth. A receding hairline that made his forehead look like it was aiming for the ceiling. I was kind of dazed, but he didn't care about that. He stared at me in a way that I didn't care for at all.

"Who are you?" he spat. I wasn't prepared for that question. I didn't know what to say. The fucker knew exactly who I was. He'd threatened to kill me a couple of weeks ago, a threat that now looked maybe less empty than it had at the time.

"Who—are—you?" he said again. Slower. But the same words. I thought that I'd better answer.

"Martin Valpolicella. Licensed private investigator. As if you didn't know."

"Martin . . . Valpolicella . . . ." He seemed to be chewing my name, tasting it, trying to fit it into something. His eyeballs went for a wander, then came home. He looked as if he was fucked up on some strange drug. He stared at me again.

"And . . . why are you here . . . Martin Valpolicella . . . ?"

"Kind of a long story, Mister Barry Eliot . . . . But I guess you know all about that, seeing as you were the bastard who fucking well set me up in the first place! For sleeping with your wife, who you've got tied to a fucking table out there! You crazy . . . ."

My voice died away. I gave up. I couldn't think of anything to call him. I had some words, sure. But they weren't enough. Anyway, even if they had been enough they wouldn't have done any good. Barry was smiling, leering, his pupils huge.

"Your words mean nothing in this place. But you are here. And you are here for a reason. And I know that reason. You do not. Whatever you think, whatever you have constructed in your mind, whatever history you have invented for yourself—is irrelevant. There is only one thing that you need to know. One thing only. Do you understand?"

I shrugged, then nodded, or something. Whatever.

"What happens to you here is forever."

He turned and walked towards the opening that led to the chamber. I wanted to say something, but no words would come. He was gone. I was alone, strapped to the stone chair. What the hell was he on about? I didn't understand. But I knew I was in trouble. A whole lot of trouble.

I tested the bonds that held me to the chair. Maybe there'd be some slack. No dice. I wasn't going anywhere. When I stopped struggling the enormity of the horror that faced me came rushing through my mind. Pigs. Clones. And Karen, out in the chamber, strapped to that infernal altar as securely as I was strapped to this goddamn chair.

I started to sweat—a freezing cold sweat that pricked my skin and ran down my forehead and burned like frost in my eyes. I fought with the fear, and I almost lost. But not quite. Okay, so this was the tightest spot I'd ever been in. But I wasn't ready to give in. Not yet, anyway. Feverishly I tried to come up with some sort of plan.

Then Stonehenge sauntered in. Looking pretty goddamn pleased with himself. He walked around me a couple of times. Then he stopped behind me. It was irritating, but I didn't try to turn my head. No point.

"I hope you're feeling fit and strong," he said quietly. "Full of beans. Ready for anything."

I didn't bother to say anything. There were a lot of things I could have said, and the choicest words were bubbling up in my throat, but I kept it all back. I figured that the more energy I kept hold of the better chance I had of getting out of this situation.

"And I hope you're not squeamish."

It was getting harder to keep silent. Squeamish?

"Oh, and that you're not bothered by the sight of blood. The smell of blood."

Not liking the sound of something had become second nature to me. Normal, even. But I definitely didn't like the sound of this at all. But I still didn't say anything. Stonehenge made a dismissive kind of noise through his nose, and walked out. So. I was alone again. The chanting continued out in the chamber. Nothing was making any kind of sense. I decided to wait until it did. I didn't have to wait long.

Stonehenge had only been gone a couple of minutes before Kafka, one of the Murnau creatures, and a Robinson came in. Behind them were two versions of the sleazebags who'd left me face down in a field by the motorway. I wondered idly if there was a clone of Kafka somewhere. Whatever. Kafka seemed to be in charge. He was, well, swaggering, or at least attempting to. But he was potentially my only ally in this mess. I couldn't figure this out. Was he acting? Or, playing a double game, double-acting? I was going to have to get him alone, to engineer the situation so that the clones would leave us alone. It was time to break my silence.

"Nice place, Colin," I said. "What's the word? *Salubrious?* Very salubrious. I like the way the ceiling drips so much. Ever thought of supplying your friends with umbrellas? Or maybe raincoats." Not rapier-sharp, but the best I could do.

"Funny. I'm laughing. *Ha. Ha.* You've got a very important role here, Valpolicella. You're very important. I realise that you're not used to being important, but we'll let that slide."

"What are you saying, Colin?"

"You're going to perform the sacrifice."

I closed my eyes. This was bad. Very bad. This was not cool. And nor was I.

"They want me to kill Karen?"

Kafka nodded, slowly. And smiled. Not a pretty sight. His mouth made a smiling shape, but his eyes bored straight into mine. The other creeps were—what were they doing? They were making a low humming noise. *Hmmmmmmmmm* . . . . Expressionless. Mouths closed. Very nearly imperceptible. And, given the situation, pretty sinister. Pretty fucking spooky.

"Colin, for fuck's sake tell those bastards to stop humming. It's starting to annoy me. Tell them to get out. I want to talk to you about this. Alone." My voice sounded kind of strange to me. Like I was trying not to cry or something.

Kafka seemed to think for a couple of seconds. He looked a bit more human. Maybe. Then he turned and muttered something to the others. They nodded slightly, and left the room.

Neither of us spoke for a while. I sat there, strapped on to my cold chair. I looked at Colin. And he looked at me. I was running scripts through my head, super fast. Trying to figure an angle that might work. Trying to figure out whose side Kafka was on. Their side? Or maybe—maybe, just maybe mine. Maybe.

"Colin, what's the deal? What the hell is going on?" He looked back at the entrance to the chamber. No one there. We had been left alone. As he spoke, he kept darting his eyes back towards the main chamber, where the chanting droned on and on.

"Bad shit, Martin. Everything Stonehenge told you—it's true. Except about Barry and Karen. She's the sacrifice. The idea is, you do it. You perform the rite. You—you kill her. With a saw. It's horrible. Barry chose you, because Karen was having an affair with you. It's not that he cares about her, because he doesn't. She's expendable. Well, she is now. He's been taking her eggs from her ovaries since just after they were married. He used to be a surgeon—but the stuff Stonehenge told you about her storing his sperm, well, she's not been using him . . . he's been using her. They use the eggs to make clones. Take an egg, add a couple of chromosomes, and bingo. They accelerate development, and within a year . . . more AFFA disciples, who never question anything, who believe in the ultimate power of AFFA—which really does mean '*nothing*,' by the way. But something about the process he's been using has gone wrong. She's become infertile. No more eggs. And then, at the same time, AFFA need a sacrifice. Karen's not productive any more, and . . . well. AFFA need more eggs. Barry needs a new wife. You can guess how They'll play it. His present wife, Karen, is found brutally murdered. Barry gets loads of sympathy, gets married again after a decent interval. AFFA really need eggs. *They're all men*, in case you hadn't noticed."

I sat there for a minute, taking it all in. But I still didn't know what I needed to know.

"Colin. Are you on my side?"

"You kill Karen. Her body is found, Barry informs his friends in the police top brass, you're arrested, everything goes to plan. AFFA really are controlling the world, Martin. More and more."

"Whatever. Are you avoiding the fucking question? *Are you on my side?*"

"I've lied to you so much, about so much . . . . I pretended to be freaked out down here, pretending that I didn't know what was going on . . . . I've been involved with this for quite a while. I was just researching weird stuff, occult stuff, hidden local history about the city, and then—well, I was approached. I admit I was scared. But they played it as if—as if I could either be with them or not. And if not, I'd lose my job. For starters. I might have an accident, you know? But it's disgusting. I'm supposed to go out there and watch while you butcher Karen with a power saw. Saw her up, alive. It's foul, depraved fucking shit, Martin."

"We can get out of this, Colin. We can. You've got a gun. You know the layout of these tunnels. We can do it. We've got to get out. That's all I want to do. We can worry about AFFA later. I just want to see the sky. Even if it's pouring with rain. Did you say *power saw*? Shit."

Kafka was looking down at the ground. He'd been looking at it for a while. He was scraping the toe of his shoe across the black slime on the flagstones, making shiny arcs on it. I waited for him to respond. I got a little hypnotised by the movement of his toe and what it did to the mould.

"I wanted to help you. In the café. I tried to warn you off."

I couldn't remember. I couldn't. Did he? "Yeah, Colin. You did. I was a fucking idiot. You tried, but you can try again. Now. Right now. Have you got the gun on you?"

"I tried to help you. I tried to stop you."

"Cool. I know. But you've got to help me again. For the last time, I promise."

"But you walked into it. Because you wanted to. Because your life was so ordinary. You wanted to be exciting. *A private investigator*, for fuck's sake. As if that job hasn't always been a load of crap. Chasing errant husbands for neurotic wives, or errant wives for neurotic husbands. Hassling debtors and defaulters. You really are a low-rent Philip Marlowe. Trying to live in a fiction. Trying to romanticise an overdraft. We wrote you the script. It landed on your doormat. And you fucking loved it. You stupid, stupid, mindless fuckwit."

This wasn't sounding too great. Kafka had a point, for sure, but I wasn't sure it was strictly relevant right now. I knew he was my only chance. But I was losing him. I needed to bring him back.

"Colin! I don't care if you've lied, or if you tried to warn me out of this mess and I ignored you. It doesn't fucking matter. Look at me, Colin. I'm strapped to a freezing cold stone chair in a little cave sixty feet under the ground, and a gang of maniac cloned freaks are about to make me kill the woman I love. Help me. Do me a favour. Please."

"You really love her?" muttered Kafka to the flagstones. Then he said it again, louder.

"You *really* love her?"

I nodded. I really did love Karen, even if I hadn't admitted it to myself until that moment. I looked at Kafka. Imploringly. I hate to say it, but that's the way I looked at him. He lifted his head. And he laughed at me. He laughed in my face. Then Barry walked in, smiling his sick sadistic smile, his words like poison in my ears.

"I'm so *glad* you love her. Very glad. Tonight, you will sacrifice her on the altar of AFFA. Your love will make the sacrifice more powerful. For lovers to kill . . . for one lover to murder the other, that is perfect. Most powerful. You are lovers. You are the killer. She is your victim."

Frantic, I looked at Kafka. He made some sort of sick attempt at a smile, raised his eyebrows, and shook his head sadly.

"You are the killer. She is your victim," he repeated, before turning round and walking out. He didn't look back.

"I've been listening to your conversation with Colin Kafka," said Barry. His voice was silky smooth, his eyes staring, his presence seeping into my soul. Listening to him was like being smothered by a satin pillow soaked with cold sweat. "I *so* enjoyed your struggling attempts to persuade him to help you. Hopeless. There is no chance of escape. You will perform the sacrifice. If you decide not to, you will be thrown into the oubliette. Do you know what an oubliette is? It's a hole. A very deep, very deep hole. Like a well. We will break your limbs, every one. We will throw you into the oubliette below the altar. You'll be alive. But you won't be alone. There are others down there. They are no longer 'alive' in the traditional sense, but . . . alive with maggots. Alive with corruption. Heaving with parasitic life. And you will lie there, in unbearable pain, waiting for the Fleet Pigs to come from the tunnels that radiate from the bottom of the oubliette. They will start to eat you alive. But they won't kill you. Oh no, they're *very* well trained. They'll leave you there on the heap of rotting bodies. You'll be alive. But not for very long, I shouldn't think. But long enough. Long enough for you to be very, very sorry that you weren't more *obedient*. It is your choice. You perform the sacrifice, or . . . . *What happens to you here is forever.* Everything is by fate ordained. And now it is time."

He made a sort of gesture in the air and a couple of Robinsons came in. And a pair of each of the kidnap-motorway-kicking guys followed them. The Robinsons moved towards me. I struggled in the chair, but it was hopeless. They walked right up and started unbuckling the straps that held me down. They came loose but there was no time to fight, or even to start to fight. I was helpless. Six men were taking care of any inclination to resist that I might have had. They started dragging me out of the room, into the chamber. I felt very sad, all of a sudden. Very sad. But I didn't cry. It wouldn't have done any good. I didn't have a plan any more. I didn't have anything. They dragged me out into the chamber, where the CCTV monitors flickered and the huge vats of dry-cleaning fluid bubbled. Where Karen lay strapped to the altar.

CHAPTER 23

THEN YOU WILL REMOVE
HER HEAD

They led me forward. Stonehenge stepped towards me. He was resting a three-foot wide wooden box on both forearms. It didn't have a lid. My head was forced down to look inside the box. It was lined with black velvet. Inside was a big power saw made of some silvery metal. It was very clean. The teeth on the circular blade looked very sharp. There was a wooden handle. A broad, curved trigger.

Stonehenge, still holding the box, turned and walked slowly towards the altar. The others were chanting and humming. I was made to follow him. He stopped right in front of Karen, whose eyes were staring wildly at me, at Stonehenge, and at the box. Whimpering sounds were escaping from behind her gag. There was a small set of steps rising to the foot of the altar. I was pushed up them. And I stood there, shaking, looking down at Karen. The bastards around me were chanting, "*Oubliette . . . oubliette . . . oubliette . . . .*" Someone pushed my head to one side. I looked down, past Karen, past the altar, down at the floor. I could see the side of a circular hole underneath the altar. Someone directed the beam of a light down the hole. I could see . . . something down there . . . bones . . . limbs . . . I tore my eyes away.

"*Oubliette . . . oubliette . . . oubliette . . . by fate ordained . . . .*"

I looked wildly around the chamber. All the hundreds of CCTV monitors were frozen, showing my face. The vats bubbled horribly in the green light that poured up through them. And AFFA stood in a circle around me and Karen and Stonehenge. Filthy water dripped like rain.

"*Oubliette . . . oubliette . . . memvola sintrompo . . . memvola sintrompo . . . .*"

Stonehenge turned to Barry, who had walked forward from the circle. Barry lifted the saw from the box. Stonehenge joined the circle. Barry stood at the head of the altar, staring at me with blank, dead eyes. Then the chanting stopped. Barry spoke in a low monotone.

"First you will remove her right arm. Then you will remove her left arm. Then you will remove her left leg. Then you will remove her right leg. Then you will make a deep incision from her stomach to her chest. And then . . . then you will remove her head."

The chanting and the humming began again. Karen's eyes were wide with terror. This was worse than any hell I could imagine. I felt paralysed. The chanting filled my mind. The vats bubbled intensely. Barry moved closer, looking directly into my eyes, and held the saw out to me.

To my utmost horror, my arms lifted involuntarily to take it from him. I looked crazily from one arm to the other. These were *my* arms! I tried to resist, but somewhere the connections between my mind and my muscles had been broken. My body had been hijacked. My arms had defected. They were nothing to do with me, they had become the arms of a puppet—AFFA's puppet!

Screaming with anguish, in a fury against my rebellious body, I raised the saw above my head, and my fingers must have gently squeezed the trigger. The saw purred, then roared into horrible life above me. I stared down at Karen, shaking my head from side to side. No! This couldn't be happening!

The chanting grew louder and louder, and I could feel dozens of eyes burning into me. The clean, sweet smell of chloroethylene was palpable. The vibration of the saw ran down my arms and throbbed in my head. The bastards were fucking with my mind! They were controlling my body! They were going to make me saw Karen apart *while she was alive*, while she could see and feel what was happening to her! First her arms, then her legs, then . . . plunging the roaring, whirling blade into her torso! Then severing her head! No! No one could do this! It was inhuman, barbaric!

And now my arms were lowering the saw . . . . I could feel the terrible weight of it. The chanting was deafening. My arms were in front of me, both hands squeezing the trigger, holding the gleaming power saw at arm's length, the sharp teeth of the saw invisible as the blade spun at high speed. Karen was struggling madly against the straps, her head threshing from side to side, a high shrieking noise coming from her gagged mouth.

With a frantic effort I closed my mind to the chanting, to the screaming saw, to *everything*. I focused on Barry, on Stonehenge, on Kafka—on AFFA. If AFFA *meant* nothing, AFFA *were* nothing! I *could* beat them.

And then, with an effort of will I didn't know I had, I did it—I broke their control over me.

My muscles grinding, tearing, I held the spinning blade inches from Karen's right shoulder. AFFA were oblivious; chanting in unison, unseeing—and I moved the saw—I sliced the whirling sawblade through the straps that bound Karen to the altar. I'd done it in an instant. Then I leapt down and held the power saw at the bastards nearest to me, waving it slowly from side to side. Barry was looking around at the others, a crazy expression on his fat face. Stonehenge was looking back at him, shaking his head furiously, his eyes wide.

"Get the fuck away! Get back!" I screamed. All of my anger was back. It was alive, and it churned into a desire for pure violence. I was getting the hell out of there, and I was going to take Karen with me. Without looking at her, I grabbed her arm and pulled her down from the altar. She tore the gag from her mouth. I held her behind me, scanning the chamber for Kafka. Then I saw him.

"Kafka! Bastard!" Still holding Karen, I edged towards him. He cowered back.

"Come here!" I bellowed over the howl of the saw. "Throw me my gun, *you lying bastard*! Now!"

Out of the corner of my eye I noticed one of the Murnaus and some of the others moving towards me. I was a metre away from Kafka, the blade aimed at his chest. He threw his gun. Karen snatched it up from the flagstones. She pointed it at a few of them while I turned around and made a lunge at the ones trying to sneak up behind us. I got Murnau's hand with the saw. One of the versions of Murnau, anyway. Some fingers came away. There was some blood. Some screaming. I didn't care. Anyway, the slicing seemed to make the rest of the fuckers a little more cautious.

I waved the saw around some more. Karen swung the gun round the chamber, holding it in both hands. And then she pulled the trigger. And a version of Robinson went down onto his knees, howling with pain. I didn't look too carefully, but there was blood almost instantly. A belly shot. That particular version of

Robinson wouldn't be much use any more. Shooting the bastard seemed to release something in Karen. She started firing all over the place. She got a little crazy, I guess. She hit a few of them, and she was screaming as loud as the AFFA guys who crumpled to the the floor. Louder, maybe. As far as I could tell, she got the other Robinson, the Murnau who still had all his fingers, and a couple of bastards I didn't know. I got the impression she was looking for Barry. But he was gone.

Pretty soon the rest of them were gone, too, running off along one of the tunnels. Karen started following them, still shooting. I yelled at her to stop. And I realised my finger was still curled tight on the trigger of the power saw, so I let go. Karen stopped shooting down the tunnel and turned towards me.

There was silence, except for the quiet bubbling of the chloroethylene vats. And a subdued whimpering sound, which I couldn't pinpoint at first. It was coming from behind my lips. Luckily they were clamped shut pretty tight.

"What the hell are *you* doing here?" asked Karen. I looked at her in some kind of shock. She was pointing the fucking gun at *me*.

"Wait," I said. "Please don't point that thing at me." I was still holding the saw, so I dropped it to the floor. She nodded upwards. I understood. So I raised my hands, very slowly.

"So?" she asked again. "What *are* you doing here, Martin? Is this another trick?"

"It's not a trick," I replied as calmly as I could. I tried to keep my voice steady. I don't remember how successful I was. "The bastards suckered me. I thought . . . ah, hell. I thought a lot of crap. Stonehenge and Kafka . . . ."

Karen was looking blankly at me, a little crease between her eyebrows. She was as beautiful as ever. If a little distraught.

"Who is *Stonehenge* and who's *Kafka*? Come on. Convince me that this isn't a trick and I won't shoot you. I don't want to shoot you. But I might have to."

I sighed. My hands were starting to go a little numb. "I was set up. I was deceived. They told me a lot of lies. They told me I was going to be arrested for murder. They enticed me down here—I didn't know what was going on, I thought—well, never mind what I thought. It'd take too long to explain. But honestly. This is not a trick. Can I put my hands down now?"

She thought about it for a second. Then she nodded. She lowered the gun. But it was still aiming roughly in my direction, I noticed.

"I don't know what's true any more," she groaned. "They told me so many crazy things . . . Barry . . . he told me that they'd used my eggs, *my eggs*, from my *ovaries*, for God's sake, to make clones . . . . They were controlling my mind, or something . . . it was ludicrous, but . . . ." She tailed off, still looking at me.

"Can I trust you?"

I nodded. "You can trust me. You might not find it easy, but it's true. I'm the only fucker you *can* trust. And we've got to get the fuck out of here. But first . . . ."

I picked the silver power saw up from the floor and walked over to the altar. Without looking down, I dropped the thing down into the oubliette. I turned back to Karen.

"I don't know about my mind, but those bastards were controlling my body. No idea how. But I came . . . close . . . to using that fucking saw on you. I'm so sorry."

"I thought that was the end. I thought you were with them, that you were one of them . . . I couldn't believe it. When I saw you here, it was—the worst part."

I looked at her. She was still in her work clothes. But they were muddy now, and torn. I could see red weals on her wrists where she'd been strapped to the altar. I walked up to her and we embraced, but clumsily. It was—awkward.

"We've got to get out of here . . . " I muttered, breaking away. I couldn't escape the thought that I had betrayed Karen. I had *believed* the lies that AFFA had told me. And I had put something inside the space between us. Something like broken glass. Or terrible thorns. Karen didn't know what it was, or why it was there, but she could feel it, too. Something vital that had worked for both of us was broken, and I had no idea if it could be mended.

"Do you know the way out?" she asked. I shook my head.

"I have no idea. But I got in. So we . . . can get out." I spoke with a confidence I didn't feel. Karen passed me the gun.

"You'd better take this, Martin," she said. "I think I've used it enough for now. I probably wasted a lot of bullets."

I looked around the chamber and tried to remember which tunnel I'd been led in through. I was pretty sure I chose right. I wasn't too bothered though. At least, we weren't going to be heading down the one the surviving members of AFFA had escaped along. Right. For sure. I walked over to one of the corpses on the floor. I rolled it over with my foot, rummaged around, and found a flashlight in a pocket.

"Come on," I said. "I think this is the right one." I passed the flashlight to Karen. I took a last glance around the chamber. There were five bodies twisted on the cold flagstones. Pity it wasn't more.

"Any idea how many of them there are?" asked Karen.

"There were twenty-three. Minus five, now." I pointed at the bodies on the bloodied flagstones. "Eighteen left. And two of us. Not very good odds," I muttered.

I wondered if I'd done the right thing by getting rid of the power saw. I guessed that I had. After all, I'd nearly butchered

Karen with it. I never wanted to see it again. Anyway, I wasn't about to clamber down into a fucking oubliette full of decomposed corpses to get it. I started thinking about what weapons AFFA might have at their disposal. But I stopped thinking about that pretty quickly. It wasn't a cheerful line of thought.

We didn't talk much, back in the catacombs. We were listening. Listening for anything that wasn't water dripping or our own feet on the flagstones. Or our own breathing. Our hearts beating. Some time passed. Then some more of it did the same. A rogue thought found its way into my head.

"Do you know anything about the pigs?" I asked Karen quietly.

"What pigs?"

"Oh, um, nothing . . . ."

Eighteen of AFFA left. Two of us. One gun. And flesh-eating pigs. I wished I'd searched all the bodies in the chamber. Located some more guns. Whatever. I wasn't about to go back. Then I remembered something. I fished around in my pocket until I found something damp and papery. I pulled out Stonehenge's map.

"Hang on," I said. "Shine the flashlight on this."

"What's that?"

"A map of these tunnels," I said. "Probably no use. Probably designed to confuse. Probably wildly, deliberately inaccurate. But still—it's a map." I turned it around until I thought I had it the right way up.

"Okay . . . " I said slowly. I slid the gun into my pocket. I pointed at the map. "I think this is the chamber we just left. And I think that . . . this . . . is the chamber under Charlcombe, which is where I came in. It's the only way out that I know. There was another one, but it's got a very heavy coffin blocking it."

"What?"

"Doesn't matter. We've got to get to Charlcombe. Probably it's about a mile and a half away. If we're going in the right direction. And that's a pretty big if. But look. If we keep going along here . . . have you noticed any side tunnels from this one, so far?"

Karen shook her head, muttered, "No . . . ."

"Okay then. We follow this tunnel until we get to a turning to the right. We take that. Then we take the first left that we come to. Then, then we go straight on until we come to the third right-hand turning. Then we come to a crossroads. We take the left. Then straight on to Charlcombe. Looks like a hell of a long way. So. Right, left, third right, left."

Karen nodded again. Then she sighed. A deep, long sigh.

"And do you think we can make it?" Her voice was small. And doubtful.

"We can make it," I said. My voice sounded the same. Small, doubtful, coming from an exhausted human far below the surface of the earth, soaking wet, very cold. Very small. Very doubtful. "Let's get a move on. Right, left, third right, left, up and out."

I took the gun out of my pocket. Put the map in. We carried on. Nothing happened. We walked quickly, sometimes jogged. We found a turning to the right. Took it. Took the next left. Nothing happened. I had a terrible feeling that we could be taking turnings in this dripping nightmare of a maze forever, map or no map.

Maybe we were already dead. After all the horrors that had happened to us, this was maybe a reasonable conclusion. That we were going round and round, exhausted, maybe pursued, on and on for all eternity. In hell. Fuelled only by a glimmer of hope that we could escape. But in reality there *was* no chance. No chance of escape. *By fate ordained . . . .*

I kept the feeling to myself. It was bad enough in my head. I didn't want it getting out. Some more nothing happened. More turnings. I counted them. Fuck, it was a long way. It felt like we'd been walking for days. Weeks. And then we reached a third turning.

"Everything's been right, according to the map," I said. My voice was a harsh croak. I cleared my throat. "We can't be more than half a mile from Charlcombe. But something's been bothering me."

Karen didn't say anything. She left enough space to have asked me what the fuck was bothering me. So I told her.

"I came down here with two of those AFFA fuckers. Stonehenge and Kafka. One of them—Kafka—was even an old acquaintance of mine. Bastard. Wish you'd killed him. Anyway, I thought they were kosher. But *they* know that the only way out *I* know is the one we're headed for. Charlcombe. And I'm thinking that maybe, when we get there, they'll be waiting for us."

"So what are we going to do?" Karen was staring at me, a yellowish glint in her eyes from the flashlight.

I let a long breath out through my teeth.

"Don't know. Not a fucking idea. Kill as many of them as we can?"

"You . . . idiot! Why didn't you say this *before*? Give me that map."

I leant back against the wet mud of the wall while Karen inspected the map with the flashlight. Fuck it, I'd done enough already. For the first time in a while I remembered that I wanted a cigarette very badly. And a drink. But neither of them were as important to me as getting out of this place. I guess that's what being trapped in hell will do for you. Give you a sense of perspective. Put things in proportion. But I still had a good think about cigarettes.

"These markings . . . " said Karen after a few minutes had passed. Or a few hours. I didn't know.

" . . . they look like they could be exits. Have a look."

I had a look. She was right. They could have been exits. They could have been anything else, too. Three dots in red could mean a lot of things. But I liked the idea that the dots marked places we could get out. There was one that seemed to be close to where we stood. If we were where we thought we were. Karen wanted to check it out. So did I. And that's what we did.

And it was a mistake.

CHAPTER 24

ROPE

Anything else would have been a mistake. Everything else would have been a mistake. We followed the map. There were a few turnings we took, and the tunnels got a little narrower. Darker. I'd got used to the occasional clouds of sulphurous fog, but even they seemed to be denser. And then we came to the place marked with the three dots on the map.

It was a small round chamber, much smaller than the one under Charlcombe. But I remembered the size of that one being different each time I'd descended into it. What was that all about? More mind control? Or did the tunnels really change size and shape? Whatever. It wasn't relevant.

The chamber we'd come to was probably big enough for about five people. Very high ceiling, though. Too high to see. There were no other tunnels from it, just the one we'd entered from. It didn't go anywhere. But there was a rope hanging down, slick and wet, running with water, suspended exactly in the centre of the circular chamber.

"Rope," I said numbly. Was this the way out?

"How far down do you think we are?" asked Karen.

"Not sure. At least sixty feet. Probably more." Even if it was fifty feet, or forty, it was going to be tough climbing a soaking rope. What bothered me was the lack of light from wherever it was that the rope was anchored. It could lead to another level of catacombs. But at least we'd be closer to the surface. It was possible that Stonehenge didn't realise I had the map. Or that he'd forgotten. The rope was our only chance. We had to take it.

"Do you want to go first?" I asked Karen. I was being practical. If she fell, she'd knock me off. Land on me at the bottom. It might kill me. That would be okay. Landing on me might save her. That was okay, too. She nodded. She grabbed hold of the rope.

And as it took her weight there was a sudden glare of greenish light. And the walls of the chamber grew away from us. And two tunnels opened like terrible mouths from the pulsating mud walls as they oozed back over flagstones slick with mould.

And people emerged from both tunnels, walking towards us.

And the people were AFFA.

And they were all carrying grey power saws.

And they walked into the growing, green-lit chamber in pairs.

And they filed in, taking positions around the walls of the now huge chamber.

And then, the last of the cabal, Barry Eliot, walked in. He held a golden power saw in his hands. And as I stared, open-mouthed, I heard Karen screaming. She was attached to the rope, as if she was *glued* there by her hands. She couldn't let go. She hung from her arms, her feet dangling pathetically a foot from the floor. Helpless. And all around me, holding saws aimed at me, AFFA laughed. They laughed. All of them. In unison. Soullessly. Laughing.

And Barry walked forward.

And he pulled on the trigger of the gold power saw.

And it purred, then roared, as he advanced towards Karen's suspended body. He raised the saw. I knew exactly what he was going to do. AFFA stopped laughing. Barry moved closer, the saw howling in his hands.

And there was only one thing I could do.

I pointed my gun. And I put a bullet through Karen's head.

CHAPTER 25

THE END

It doesn't matter what happened after that. Nothing I had done had made any difference to anything. I had never been in control. I had never been anything other than an amusing puppet. *By fate ordained.* It was Monday 13th July.

I'm sitting on the edge of the bed in my flat. I'm waiting for the police to arrive. They're going to charge me with Karen's murder.

And as I sit here, I can see out of my window. It's stopped raining. And I think the sun's going to come out. Yeah. Well.

ABOUT THE AUTHOR

Stanley Donwood (the pen name of Dan Rickwood) is best known for being the "in-house" illustrator for Radiohead, having created all of their album and poster art since 1994. Donwood's other works of fiction include *Slowly Downward* and *Household Worms*, both published by Tangent, and *Humor*, a collection of old and new work, published by Faber.